Showdown at Emerald Canyon

Also by Jeff Clinton

EMERALD CANYON

Showdown at
Emerald Canyon

JEFF CLINTON

DOUBLEDAY & COMPANY, INC.
GARDEN CITY, NEW YORK
1975

20739

All of the characters in this book are fictitious,
and any resemblance to actual persons, living or
dead, is purely coincidental.

Library of Congress Cataloging in Publication Data

Bickham, Jack M
Showdown at Emerald Canyon.

I. Title.
PZ4.B584Sk [PS3552.I3] 813'.5'4
ISBN 0-385-01890-8
Library of Congress Catalog Card Number 74-15782

Showdown at Emerald Canyon

ONE

A hot dry wind blew down the length of Emerald Canyon. In the northern sections it parched the earth and forced the farmers there to haul water nightly in their dilapidated wagons, for irrigation, and in the town of Emerald Canyon it kicked up dust devils in the streets and sifted around window casings and made men squint against its cruelty. Even in the southern reaches of the canyon, where the river made the land kinder, it turned tree leaves brown here and there as it whistled along, biting, sucking life out of the things it touched, including men. There had seldom been a harsher September than this one of 1873, and some said you could look for trouble when the weather was like this because men's tempers grew short when the wind blew hot and dry.

Surrounded by massive land holdings and overlooking a broad sweep of the Emerald River, Samuel Kane's great house stood bleak against the wind, seemingly untouched by it. Built by more than a dozen expert carpenters and stonemasons over a period of two years, it reflected the stolid tastes and enormous power of the former cattle baron who had opened the valley for settlement. Nothing could touch Sam Kane's house, people said. It was a fortress against weather, against men, against change.

There were two carriages parked in front of the house this day, although the dusty wind made it a bad one for travel. They stood near the great, pillared front porch.

Inside the house, in the dining room, the sound of the gritty wind could not penetrate. The giant room was very still, although three men sat at the table, waiting. Middle-aged, dark-suited, morosely smoking cigars, they betrayed their tensions by furtive looks at one another. None had ever been summoned by Sam Kane unless it was some kind of crisis. Now they knew only in the most general way what the crisis was.

Double oak doorways at one end of the room swung open sharply, creating a little gust of wind that stirred the candles in the chandelier. A short, stout man, red-faced and with the stubble of beard on his cheeks, strode in. He walked to the head of the table, pulled out a gold pocket watch, consulted it, and leaned heavy hands on the edge of the table.

"Gents, I appreciate you all coming on short notice. Hope the ride out wasn't too danged blustery."

One of the men stirred, put down his cigar in a silver ashtray. "No problem at all, Sam. You know that."

Sam Kane smiled bleakly at the man who had spoken. He knew Henry Strider detested travel on dusty, windy days; Strider always left on-site inspections for his land company to subordinates on days like this, staying inside his town office and hugging his charts and amortization schedules. But Henry Strider knew which side his bread was buttered on, just as the others did.

Purposefully, Kane turned to each of the other men in turn, testing their attitude also. "Everything all right at the company, Tom? Anything unusual going on at the bank, H.R.?"

Thomas S. Simmons, major owner of Simmons Feed and Produce Company, and a Kane business partner in several other operations, raised his thinly aristocratic profile. "You know the problems, Sam."

"But you're making out," Kane told him, still probing.

"Well, things have changed. You know that, of course."

"But you're making out."

"Well . . . yes."

Kane turned his eyes. "H.R.?"

Bulky, gray, H. R. Yeager watched Kane warily for an instant before answering. "Nothing unusual."

"You're making out, too, then," Kane said.

"I guess you could say that."

"Would *you* say that?"

Yeager frowned uncomfortably.

There was a moment of silence.

Kane raised his flattened hands slowly, then brought them down on the table with explosive force. The sound was like a gunshot. Yeager, Strider, and Simmons jumped a foot.

"Gents," Kane said in the same deceptive tone, "things are *not* all right. We are *not* making out. Everything we've built is going to hell in a hand basket. I'm sick of it!"

The three partners stared silently at him. He could see whites of their eyes all the way around the irises.

He told them derisively, "Let me just tell you what's happening. Number one, the balance of political power is in danger of shifting. Number two, our entire basic operating policy on managing the economy in Emerald Canyon is coming apart at the seams. Number three, the land development program is on high center. Number four—well, to hell with number four; the first three things are bad enough. They take in just about everything we've tried to build here, gents. We are losing our butts."

Kane paused and allowed the crude word to hang in the air. He had begun only half in earnest, intending to build them up for the things that had to be decided. But his words had unleashed just a little of the real agony and frustration inside him, and now it was boiling out truly, carrying him as well as them along with it.

"You don't make progress by trying to stand still," he told them, and began pacing back and forth, arms locked behind his back. "When I bought my first cows, to take up the trail, some big men down there said I was crazy. By God, I took those cows through drought and then flood, and twisters—Indians, thieves, you name it. But we took them through. That's the way you build. You don't build a thing by sitting back, saying how hard it might be.

"I'll tell you how a winner looks at things. You stand an ordinary man up to a brick wall, he'll just sit down, or start thinking of a way to get around. But a man that's got guts, that wants it bad enough, why, he'll just go right *through* the goddamned thing, because that's the way a real man—a winner—is.

"You know what they told me when I came to Emerald Canyon? They told me the same thing they told me when I started the herds up the Goodnight-Loving Trail. 'You can't make it,' they said. 'That's sacred Indian ground,' they said. 'Nobody could make that canyon into a profitable venture,' they said. *'Quit,'* they said."

Kane balled his fists and glared at the other men. "There's just one thing I know how to do, you know. It ain't listen and it ain't quit. I just got one thing and that's a hard head. All I can do, when I want something, is fight you until one of us is dead.

"So that's how I am and that's how I like myself. And pardon me, gents, if I don't take it too kindly, to have you come in here and say we're making it all right when we're losing our butts."

Thomas S. Simmons raised frightened eyes. "Sam, you're the one who said we had to take it easy . . . try to ride this trouble out."

"I said that in July," Kane shot back. "This is September."

"Yes, but—"

"I'm going to review for you," Kane cut in. "As of just a couple or three months ago, we didn't have a bad deal here. I'm not going to go into all the business tie-ins you gents have with me and each other, or about some of the deals we've worked with others that aren't here today. But two of the main things we had going were the land business and the loans.

"We promoted land in the north end of the canyon. Nothing wrong with that. We sold and made loans, and got families in from the East. We sold land, loaned 'em the money. Nothing wrong with that, either.

"Water was scarce up there in the summer. A lot of those people would stay a few months, go broke, get foreclosed on, move out. That's the law. That's nature taking its course. If we took the land back and sold it again to somebody else— giving some new settler a chance to try *his* luck—that wasn't wrong. That was giving people their chance. If they could stay, and be lucky, they were welcome.

"On top of that, of course, we had the market in the canyon. Between us, we controlled food sales, feed, all of it. We ran it clean. We made a decent profit, but there's nothing wrong with that, either. It's the American way, always has been. We just got done fighting a war so men could make their own way and have a decent profit."

Kane paused, scratched furiously at his scalp, and resumed pacing. "When our town marshal died last summer, naturally we wanted a good man. That's good for business and prosperity, having a strong law, even though we always kept things quiet in the canyon with the law or without. So we brought in this Jim Bradley."

"That's when our troubles started, all right," Henry Strider sighed.

Kane silenced him with a look. "I accept the responsibility for most of that. I was the one that wanted Bradley. I'd heard he was tough. But I thought he'd be ready to settle down, listen to reason.

"All right. We brang him, installed him. But then he started this whole thing of working with the dirt farmers. Helped those rabble-rousers, that German named Schmitz and the other one, McCollum, organize them an agricultural cooperative. Wouldn't run them off when their loan notes were due. Protected them on their first trips to the river with those damned water wagons, for irrigation.

"You remember what happened to Abe McCune. He tried to stop them direct. Damned fool went crazy. Ended up dead, right? Made Bradley a hero all over the canyon, instead of the opposite, right? That's what happens when you attack some problems head on. And that's why I said we would wait, back there in July. I thought Bradley might fritter away his popularity quick-like, or the farmers would fail anyhow. I didn't want to wait, it's not my nature. But with Bradley knowing about a lot of our deals and partnerships, we had to wait . . . then."

Kane paused again, glaring at them, hating them for their weakness that always required him to start everything. "But that was July. This, like I said, is September."

"Maybe," Simmons said softly, "we can still ride it out, Sam. We haven't been hurt too badly yet, and—"

Kane's hands slammed on the table again. "How bad do you have to be hurt before you know it, Tom? Do you have to have your guts hanging out, and be *dead?*"

"Oh, it isn't that bad," Yeager gasped. "We're collecting a tidy profit as the farmers make their payments on time, and—"

"And food prices have gone to hell," Kane cut in, "as them farmers haul in their irrigated produce and sell it under what we want to maintain as fair pricing. And our land deals are at a standstill. And now they've made their first haul *out* of the canyon, to Ferndale, and turned a neat profit there, too.

"You don't maintain your power by trying to stand still, gents. We been trying that and it hasn't worked. It never will work. *Never.* And now this latest thing is coming on us."

He waited for one of them to ask.

After a few seconds, Yeager did so. "New thing, Sam? I don't know if I know what you're talking about."

"Political power," Kane snapped.

"But we control the town board, and always have."

"There's an election in November, or did you forget?"

Yeager looked startled. "Henry and Tom, here, and Bailey —they'll run just as before—"

"The farmers are going to put up a slate," Kane told them. His words were quiet now, because he had known what effect the news would have. He was not disappointed. The impact was quietly brutal. The men went slack-faced, then a dirty gray. Strider's cigar fell out of his mouth and bounced off his lap in a shower of sparks that he quickly and frantically began beating out.

"They wouldn't have a chance!" Yeager said.

"My information," Kane said heavily, is that Schmitz, the German, is going to run. And the other one. McCollum. And maybe a third man, too."

"But we've always run the town! We—"

"They're the heroes," Kane bit off. "The water deal made everybody look up to them. And they've got Bradley looking after them. He's a hero, too—and he's connected with their side in the public eye."

The silence grew thick. Kane waited for them.

Simmons finally said softly, "We just have to . . . work harder. More advertising this time. Banners. Go talk to everybody. Rallies. We run the newspaper, we can control—"

"We can't control anything!" Kane shot back. "That's just the point! We've already lost too much, and now we stand to lose a lot more unless we do something. A *lot* more!"

"What can we do, other than the things I mentioned?" Simmons asked.

"We can come out," Kane told them. "Fight."

"But you said—"

"We won't come out McCune's way. Not the open way. That's no good. But we're staring right down the pipe at *destruction*, gents. It's that simple. If we don't get off our butts and get busy right here and now, we're finished in this canyon —we'll have lost it."

"My God," Yeager said thickly. "We'll have to have a full meeting—"

"No," Kane said.

"What?"

"No," Kane repeated.

They stared at him.

"Too many cooks spoil the pie," Kane told them. "That's why I invited you three. There ain't going to be any more."

"Not Bailey? After all, he's on the board—"

"Not Bailey. And not Kendall. And not Luke Ball. And not anybody else. The more we get in it, the more chance there is for error. *We're* handling this, gents. The four of us."

It was symptomatic that no one even questioned Kane's judgment.

"How?" Simmons asked.

"Jim Bradley has got to be discredited. So do Schmitz and McCollum."

"I don't know how we can do that. They're heroes, practically, like you said. And there are a lot more—"

"Bradley is the law, so he's central," Kane interrupted. "Schmitz and McCollum, they lead the farmers. They're the officers of that danged co-op. Get these three and we got the power back. Let 'em go and we might as well start packing up. It's that simple."

"But *how* can we discredit any of them?"

"I've got a plan," Kane said.

They waited, obedient. In other affairs they carried great power, but here they waited like schoolchildren for the teacher to speak.

Then, however, Kane surprised them once more.

"It's dangerous," he said. "You all have to know that. I ain't forcing anybody into it. It's all of us together, or none—and we take our chances otherwise."

The other three men frowned at one another, startled by this genuine offering of some sort of democratic procedure. It was new in their dealings with Sam Kane, and it was a little frightening. If he was actually giving them a *voice*—why, then the gamble had to be desperate indeed.

Kane told them, "It's like the brick wall. If we go, we *go*. We just bust into that wall and go through, or we keep trying until we're dead. This is all or nothing, gents. Do you want to hear about it?"

Again no one spoke. The room became so quiet that the sound of Kane's expensive gold watch could be heard distinctly.

Finally Thomas S. Simmons, very pale, licked his lips and spoke. "We'll go with you on it, Sam. Whatever it is. Tell us what we have to do."

Kane turned fierce eyes on Yeager. "You agree?"

He was forcing them to buy it sight unseen. It had to be this way—total acceptance, without question. They all saw this, and this, too, was chilling.

Yeager's ox eyes rolled. "I agree. Yes."

"Henry?"

Strider swallowed hard. He nodded silently, without looking up from his clenched hands on the tabletop.

"Fine, then," Kane said huskily. "It's the four of us. Nobody else. We're going to do what we have to do, for ourselves and our associates and the future of the canyon. We're going to destroy Jim Bradley. We're going to destroy Schmitz. We're going to destroy McCollum. That's it. There ain't any other way. It's all or nothing. Here's the plan."

TWO

It was half past ten o'clock, and as usual the town of Emerald Canyon had seemed to go to sleep with the setting of the summer sun. The farmers' water wagons were moving, out on the back road to Low Point and the spot where they loaded their barrels for the long trek back to their parched fields, and here and there in town the lights of a domino parlor glowed yellow against the black. But the stores and shops along the main street were closed for the night with only a few exceptions, and the street lay virtually deserted, silent, peaceful.

In the café Jim Bradley was as usual the last customer. His routine had become set by now, after two months on the job: walk the beat, rattle doorknobs as twilight became full night, walk north as far as the feedstore and south to Jenkins's Livery, go around the block east to the church, come back to Main, reach Jean Reff's café for supper a little before ten.

He was right on schedule tonight, and now had his second cup of coffee before him. Jean Reff had shuttered the windows, locked the door, finished cleaning up behind the counter, and now brought a cup of coffee of her own over to join him. She was a tall, handsome woman not so much younger than Bradley's forty-six years, although many of those years had been kinder to her and she looked, to him, very much younger indeed.

She sat down stiffly and grimaced. "Oof." She rubbed her back.

"Poor old lady," Bradley grinned.

"I've had a day."

"I noticed the line at noon."

"Everyone in town decided to eat here today."

"Don't put up the 'homemade pie' sign if you want any peace and quiet," Bradley advised.

She made a face of mock surprise. "Is that what it was?"

"That," he told her, "and the pot roast. And the bread. Oh, and I heard somebody bragging about your blue plate today, too."

"I guess I shouldn't complain. Business has picked up faster than I could have dreamed."

"You're a good cook. Among other things."

Her pretty eyes darted to his face. "Among other things?"

It was as close as he could skirt toward an outright compliment. She made him too uncomfortable for more than that. He changed the subject a little. "Of course the town is sort of prosperous right now, too."

She allowed him to make the switch. "I know a lot of the so-called old guard thought it would be the end of the world when the Yank farmers started hauling their produce. But it certainly has changed the look of the spending public—revitalized things."

"They're just getting a good start," Bradley told her. "Another shipment goes out near the end of the week."

"I wouldn't have believed that a few months ago, either."

"The farmers are together now. That's what's making things work."

"Don't you think," Jean Reff asked, "you deserve a little credit, too?"

Bradley shrugged. "They've mostly done it themselves."

"Sometimes you sell yourself short. Do you know that?"

"Not really, Jean."

She made a fist at him. "It's true. You've been the difference. Why do you pretend otherwise? You should be proud of the things you've accomplished!"

Bradley smiled at her. "I'm a fairly good lawman. I know that."

"Fairly good! Honestly!"

"It's true," he said calmly. "Face it. There wasn't any real crime when I came here in July. Once a few businessmen learned I wasn't going to take sides against the poor—that it was going to be the same law for everyone—there's been no trouble at all."

"You went against the power structure," Jean Reff pointed out with quiet firmness. "It takes quite a man to do that."

Bradley drained his coffee cup. "Hey, do you want to give me the big-head, lady?"

"No, certainly not. But—"

There was a shout in the street. Bradley turned sharply to the window and saw a shadowy figure running raggedly up the street from the north end. The shout came again, sharper and closer: *"Marshal! Marshal!"*

Bradley shoved back from the table and hurried to the door, shooting the bolt open. He stepped out onto the planked porch. "Here! What is it?"

The shadowy figure skidded to a halt and Bradley recognized a man named Tuck, who owned a small feedstore near the north edge of the two-block business district.

"Come quick!" Tuck called hoarsely. "Somebody's breakin' in my place!"

Bradley turned to Jean Reff, who had come to her feet. "I'll be back."

"Be careful!" she called after him, but he was already running.

Tuck, a skinny man with graying hair, ran alongside him, explaining as well as he could, given his shortness of breath. "—was in the front, baggin' some feed—heard a noise in back —went through the back door—heard somebody with a pry bar at the freight entry."

They ran past the post office and into the deeper dark of the far north block. Bradley panted, "Did they see or hear you?"

"Don't think so—I come out runnin' to git you—"

"You did right, Tuck."

"Don't have a gun in there—"

"Hold it, now. You stay here."

They had reached the line of one-story storefronts that included Tuck's Feed. Lights all were out except in Tuck's, the fourth doorway up the way, and that door swung open onto the porch, allowing a faint shaft of light to spill outside. Winded by the short run, Bradley tried to hear sounds ahead, or see a movement. He could not discern either.

"Stay here," he repeated to Tuck. "I'm going around back."

Tuck nodded and stood his ground.

Gun in hand, Bradley edged between the buildings, moving with swift silence. The space between buildings smelled dustily of rot. It was pitch black. A rat or something was startled ahead of him and made a scurrying sound. He reached the narrow alley and turned to his right, staying close to the building walls, closing in on the patch of light that shone faintly from a dirty window in the back of the feedstore.

Getting nearer, he saw that the back door, made of heavy timbers, had been pried open about a foot. Rope ties inside prevented it from being opened farther. There was no sign of anyone, although he could make out boot-heel marks in the deep dust around the doorway outside.

Pressed against the wall, he listened. The building seemed perfectly still.

Holding his breath, Bradley slipped inside the narrow doorway opening, climbed over the security rope on the bottom and ducked under the one at the top, and looked around.

He was in the rear storage area—barrels, bags, sacks, and crates piled helter-skelter. It was dusty and dim. There was no sound. The room was not big enough to hide much of anything. Still he moved cautiously, sidling along the wall until he could get a look behind some barrels that might have hidden a crouching man.

There was no one.

Bradley eased his way to the door that led to the front

part of the store. He poked his head out and looked around. It looked empty. He waited, forcing himself to count slowly to one hundred.

He stepped out into the front portion of the store. "Anybody here?"

Silence answered him.

He walked to the counter, beginning to feel a fool. He looked under it, walked along the far wall, and poked at the sacks there. Then, breathing easier, he walked to the front door.

"Come on in!" he called softly. "Whoever it was, they're gone."

Tuck hurried up, his eyes wide with apprehension. "I swan," he muttered. "I got so scared, it being so long since *anybody* got robbed or anything around these parts—"

"You did the right thing," Bradley told him. "Somebody did try to force your back door. Did a pretty good job of it, too. They must have heard you run out."

"Guess I better get me a better rope deal back there."

"You'd better get yourself an honest brace bar, if you want my opinion."

"Well by gosh, I'll do it, Jim. I just never expected—"

A distant sound—several blocks away—broke his words off in midstride. Bradley spun toward the sounds as they came.

There were three, then two more, close together. They were unmistakable.

"What *is* that?" Tuck gasped.

"Just what you think it is," Bradley gritted, and started running again.

They had been gunshots, at least five of them and perhaps more if the reports were right on top of one another, and they had come somewhere in the vicinity of the park or the church. The sound had been extremely ugly because it was so unexpected—so out of character for Emerald Canyon. There had been nothing like this at night in his brief tenure—nothing

like the attempted break-in at Tuck's, nothing like open gunfire in the night. Was there a connection?

He pushed his legs hard, and thought fleetingly of how he
was starting to get old.

Almost a dozen people had already appeared in the square
in front of the church when he rounded the corner and ran
up to join them. Somebody had a lantern and everyone was
talking at once.

"What happened?" Bradley demanded. "What's going on?"

"We don't know, Marshal! We was all home, or in the
parlor, there, and the shots sounded and we come out to see
what it was all about!"

"There was a lot of shots!" someone else said. "Close!"

"Where, exactly?"

Several of them pointed toward the park itself, pitch black,
studded here and there with trees, built around the old fountain that didn't work anymore.

"Did any of you *see* anything?" Bradley asked.

They all looked blank-faced.

Bradley turned, cut across the street, and headed for the
park. Some of them started to follow at a distance.

"Stay back over there!" he yelled at them.

Hurrying on, he reached the dusty grass of the park. The
lantern light faded behind him, leaving a long shadow and
then going on, and he was under the trees. He had his gun
out again and he was sweating, out of breath. He couldn't
see a thing under the trees. He was far enough from the on-
lookers now that they might as well have been a million miles
away: the faint echo of their voices at a distance only in-
creased his sense of isolation.

There was no movement in the park.

He pressed deeper, nearing the center. He reached the rim
of the trees and moved into the clearing that surrounded the
old rock fountain. It was flowed from a spring once, but something had happened, and now it sat dry, dusty, clogged with
leaves and debris. Two benches stood nearby, empty.

His pores shrinking from the task, Bradley moved out of the tree cover and toward the fountain.

It put him in the open, fully visible to anyone who had been here long enough to accustom his eyes to the bright star illumination. Even though he had come so recently from the bright light of the lantern, even Bradley felt like the clearing was as bright as day. He did not like exposing himself. But this is what you did when you were the law. You couldn't send someone else. There *was* no one else.

He walked slowly to the fountain. It was still and warm in the clearing and he caught the faint, sharp odor of gunpowder. The shooting had taken place very near this spot.

He reached the fountain and looked beyond it. On the far side, the grassy area was open all the way to the far street, with its weedy fields beyond. He could see all around his position, and there was no one.

It was very strange.

Puzzled, he turned and started back the way he had come.

The attempted break-in, he could understand. Highly un-usual, but the kind of thing one had to expect every so often in any town, no matter how quiet or law-abiding.

The gunfire, however, was something else. It had no rhyme or reason for it. It made no sense at all. A prankster? A drunk? Some kids trying to stir up a little late-summer ex-citement?

Up ahead through the trees there was renewed shouting and excitement.

"Over there!" a voice sang out shrilly. "Look! *Fire!*"

Oh, my God.

Running into the street, Bradley saw where the excited crowd was looking. The fire was about two blocks away—south—and whatever it was, it was already going very heavily indeed. The crimson glow lit the sky over the black flatiron shapes of building roofs in between its location and the park.

"Somebody get the bell going in the square," Bradley or-dered. "Volunteer fire department on the run. Hurry!"

Although most of the small crowd streamed up the street toward Main, there was a more direct route to the sky glow, and Bradley took it. Heading down the side of the park, he plunged across some weed fields, intending to come out on the far side where the county road went through. It was only about three blocks this way, but more than twice that distance if he followed the streets.

The fields were lumpy and weedy, about waist-high with dry brush, and he plunged right in without thought. It was hard going, but he had to make time. As dry as everything was along the street, a fire could get out of control very easily. It might be necessary to knock a building down—construct a fire break of some kind. It all depended on what was afire. As far as the sky glow seemed to be, it had to be one of the abandoned storage sheds on the farthest edge of the town. Kids smoking, maybe. Or spontaneous combustion. Maybe it could be headed off.

Shoving through the brush, he caught a glimpse of the county road about fifty or seventy yards ahead. The town was packed in very close to its two major streets, and his shortcut, because the main street curved, had taken him several hundred yards out behind the nearest buildings. He was practically out in the country, all of a sudden, and he felt stupid again.

There was a mammoth old buffalo wallow directly ahead, and on the far side, the dusty, empty road. He started around the tufted lip of the old wallow, which was perhaps sixty feet wide at its narrowest point and about eight feet deep at the center. Running along the rim, he was intent on the road just ahead.

Something exploded and gushed orange. All sorts of bad stuff hummed past his face.

Without thought he dived head-first down the slope of the wallow. A second gunshot—it had been a shotgun at very close range—blasted the night above him. He hit and rolled over and over, wondering if he had broken his neck.

Reaching the bottom, he knew he had no time to worry about minor injuries. He came up on hands and knees and scurried wildly for the far bank, intent on circling around the point of attack. He was spitting dust, half-gagged on mouthfuls of it.

It was very hard to believe any of this was happening. Bradley knew he was fighting more than one kind of shock as he crawled up the far bank of the wallow in the pitch-blackness. You never—no matter who you were or what your experiences might have been—took a gunshot at close range without your nervous system going crazy. You were, after all, awfully close to death, and the organism reacted to this primitive knowledge in its own primitive ways. But in addition there was the factor of uniqueness for the town of Emerald Canyon. Things like this just didn't *happen* in town. Now the burglary, the shooting, the fire—and *this!*

It was not a moment, however, for trying to figure much of it out. Bradley had neared the lip of the old wallow, where tufted grass and weeds overhung the edge and formed a shaggy cover. Getting knees under himself, he moved cautiously upward, poking his head up over the brush to see what he could see.

On the far side—halfway to the road—something winked fire. Pellets buzzed overhead as he scrambled under cover of the lip again. The sound was a throaty roar, probably a 10-gauge.

Gritting his teeth, Bradley thought it over. The man over there did not have good cover of his own, had probably counted on the first shot. His position put Bradley slightly beyond optimum range for a shotgun, and if he had a single loader, he was risking a counterattack while he had his weapon open to punch in a new shell. So the attacker could not be very happy.

Bradley's position, however, was no better. He was pinned down and could not risk the possibility of a double-barrel shotgun that would give his attacker a clear second shot quickly. Also, in the poor light he was not at all sure he could make his revolver count at this range and against a mobile target.

It looked like stalemate.

But there was just one thing wrong with stalemate in this kind of game. It wasn't chess. The two pieces could not move back and forth forever, no advantage given or taken. In this situation, someone was sure to make a false move. Stalemate always degenerated when the pieces had guns.

He considered his options, none of which was very good. Rolling over on his back against the gritty steep dirt, he checked his Colt for sand that might block its action. It seemed all right. He rolled over again, braced himself, and reached into the thickly tufted brush on the lip. As carefully and slowly as he could, he pulled himself up over the lip by main strength of his arms. This kept him very low.

The other man didn't see him. There was no shot.

His heart beating hard, Bradley remained still for a minute or two. Grit stuck to his sweaty face and arms, and tension made his breathing labored. He could smell the dusty green of the brush that protected him.

Very slowly he began inching his way forward through the grass, getting an angle away from the wallow. He got into some stickers and cut his hand, but paid no attention. Minutes were inching away.

There was no signal from his attacker. Was he also maneuvering?

Bradley had gotten about fifteen feet from the edge of the wallow when he turned, still belly-down in the grass, to start a circling route toward the road and the last place he had seen the wink of the shotgun. It was eerily still. Toward town the crimson glow of the fire seemed lower, but he could still hear excited voices in the distance.

Then suddenly he heard voices much nearer—coming up the little road from the direction of town.

"I heard at least two shots, I tell you!"

"Nobody's out here! You're crazy!"

"I heard it!"

"Let's go to the fire!"

"Come on!"

"Aw!"

Two voices, young boys, excited.

Bradley raised his head slightly and incredulously spotted them coming right up the road, shadow-figures in the starlight. They were already very close. Coming fast. Walking right into it.

He made an immediate decision. *"Go back!"* he yelled.

The two figures stopped. *"What?"*

"Go back!"

"Who is that?"

There was still no sign from the attacker. Bradley risked raising his head over the grass cover. "Get back to town! You're in danger here!"

"Who is that?" one of the boys cried.

But there was nothing from the attacker.

Bradley thought he saw why.

Every nerve screaming, he raised himself deliberately into fuller view.

There was no shot—no sign of anyone but the two boys on the road.

"Who is that out there?" one of the boys piped nervously.

Bradley got to his feet, and still there was no reaction. Breathing deeper, he walked around the edge of the wallow toward the road. The two boys watched, backing up a little, ready to run.

"It's okay, fellers. It's me. Jim Bradley."

"Gosh! We was scairt! Did we hear shootin' out here?"

Bradley reached the spot near the road where the shotgun had winked at him. Bending down, he felt around the place where a man's feet had beat the grass down into a kind of hiding nest. His fingers felt something smooth and warm and he picked it up: a brass cartridge case, 10-gauge just as he had guessed. Feeling around some more, he found another just like it.

"What's going on, Marshal?" one of the boys piped up again. "You out here by yourself?"

"I am now." Bradley hid the casings from them. "Come on. We'd better get back and see about that fire."

The volunteers almost had it out when he got there. Or it might be more accurate to say the flames had already done their work. It had started in an abandoned storage shed in a vacant lot, and men were running back and forth from the little pumper with buckets, but they were by now pouring water on embers anyway. The thin roof and flimsy walls had gone fast and there was nothing left but a smoking mess of rubble.

"Durned lucky it was this one, out here by its lonesome!" a man named Simms told him excitedly. "If it'd got in that row just up the street, we'd of had us a real mess."

"Very lucky," Bradley nodded.

"I'll say so! *Real* lucky!"

"Any idea yet what started it?"

"Nope. Nobody has an idee at all. Purvis owns it. Says it was empty. How could a fire start in an empty shack like this settin' all by itself? Strange!"

Bradley watched the men continue, slower now, to pour water on the wreckage. "You'll be staying to get the last of it out?"

"Oh, right. Yes siree. Can't have any sparks left to start a bad fire down the street."

Bradley nodded agreement again and turned away. He started up the street toward the main part of town, sucking dirt out of the gash on his hand that the thorns had made. The excitement had brought a lot of people out, and many called out questions to him which he answered without much thinking about it.

Reaching Jenkins's Livery, where buildings began lining up along both sides of the street in the crowded fashion all towns seemed to encourage no matter how much land was available on all sides, Bradley left the street and cut down the narrow alley. He went the block through the alley slowly, rattling back doorknobs and checking locks with greater care. At the corner he continued on into the next block of alleys, doing the same thing.

It was all very damned peculiar. Nothing ever seemed to happen in town, and tonight *everything* had happened. It was possible that it was all coincidence. He didn't think so. Had everything been designed to get him isolated for the ambush? This seemed more likely. But who was a suspect in that case?

It was within the realm of possibility that an old enemy had returned. He had sent enough men to prison over the years. Sometimes one came back, harboring his rusty load of hate that had to be vented this way. But Bradley had not seen anyone around town who looked even faintly suspicious.

He knew that the town's elite, from Samuel Kane right on down, had plenty of motive for getting rid of him. But one of their number, a man named McCune, had tried frontal violence two months ago, during the big showdown over water rights. McCune was dead. Neither Kane nor any of his colleagues could afford an outright assault of this kind. Being the established power structure in Emerald Canyon, they stood to lose too much if violence was begun, and carried along out of hand. So this did not seem like the kind of thing they might try.

What, then?

Bradley returned to the possibility that it was all accidental. He hoped this was so. Confronted with continuing worry, however, he did about the only thing he knew how to do: he met threat with established practice, going on, checking doorknobs and windows, trying to make sure everything was secure.

It took a while.

He was almost finished up when he walked down the alley behind the town's top retail establishments. Up ahead the alley was wider where a building behind the main row had once fallen down. The area was used for dumping trash and there was an abandoned water well there, just behind Simmons Feed and Produce.

A shadowy figure suddenly moved near the round rock wall of the well. *"Who is that?"* a voice called huskily.

Bradley recognized the voice and relaxed. "Bradley," he said, and walked forward out of the deeper shadows.

Thomas Simmons, pale in rolled shirt sleeves, put down a small box of what looked like trash and audibly breathed a sigh of relief. "Scared me, Jim!"

"What are you doing out here this time of night?" Bradley asked.

Simmons mopped his forearm across his face. "With all the excitement, I thought I had better check my doors and windows."

"Out here in the alley?"

"Well," Simmons said, and then, uncharacteristically, grinned, "I knew I wouldn't be able to sleep for a while. I had this trash, I just thought I'd dump it, do some minor chores."

"I'm going along, checking doorways and windows," Bradley told him. "You don't have to worry."

"I suppose so, but golly! Everything happened at once tonight, didn't it?"

"Seemed to," Bradley agreed.

Simmons picked up the small box. "Well, guess I'll get back inside, lock up, and go home. It's almost midnight, I reckon."

Bradley said nothing as the man walked to the rear door of his building, went inside, slammed the heavy door firmly. Bradley heard the bar fall inside.

Simmons, he thought, walking on, was one of those who

would like to see him out of the marshal's job. But Simmons had been a supporter in July, had seconded the town board motion to hire him. Of course that had been before they all realized he would not be their puppet. Well, maybe it had been lucky, having Simmons see him tonight so obviously on the job. Bradley doubted it.

He finished checking doors and windows, then walked down part of the length of the street. Magically, as quickly as they had been stirred up, things were quiet again. People had mostly gone home. Lights had gone out. A soft breeze stirred and a black cat streaked across an alley, and vanished.

The light remained on behind the shades of the café.

"You're still up?" Bradley asked with some surprise when Jean Reff opened the door.

"Of course I am," she replied. "You *said* you'd be back."

"It's late. Sorry."

"We've had all kinds of excitement."

"It's fine now. Everything is calmed down."

"Anything serious? They told me the fire was minor."

"Just a little flurry," he lied.

"Come in for coffee?" she asked.

He wanted to. That was why he couldn't. "I'd better stay on the street for a while. You get to sleep, Jean."

She smiled. "Yes, master."

"See you tomorrow."

"I certainly hope so," she told him archly.

He turned away from the door after it was closed. He looked up and down his street. Without a doubt, Emerald Canyon was one of the cleanest, nicest towns he had ever known. Even in the darkness he could see all the fresh paint on storefronts, the little trees people had planted to try to dress up the spaces along the board sidewalks. People took pride here. There might not be many buildings with two stories, and they might be close together along a street that was crazily crooked in two places, giving things a slightly mixed-up look, but these were good people and they had made it a good place to live.

For a moment his imagination painted a picture that showed him an ordinary citizen, a storekeeper, perhaps, or farmer, with a family . . . Jean . . . children. Then it would truly be his town because he would be *of* it, not a guardian, not a hired hand.

But then he rejected the idea because it was too impossible.

He stepped down off the café porch into the deep dust of the street. Down at the corner, a couple of the volunteer firemen walked toward their homes, talking softly. Their voices carried in the stillness.

Bradley pulled out his gold watch. It was midnight. Three hours until Freddie Smith, his black deputy, came on duty. Many nights Bradley holed up in his office these last hours of his shift, making only cursory rounds every couple of hours or so. He decided against that routine tonight. He would stay out here, and watch, and earn his money for a change.

THREE

Bradley was awake again at 6:30 the next morning. Groggy after less than three hours' sleep, he made coffee, gnawed on a couple of stale biscuits, and left his house.

The house, a good walk south of town, was one of the job's fringe benefits; the town provided it. Ordinarily Bradley allowed himself the luxury of sleeping until about 9:30 or 10, and then another hour or so around the place before getting into town. He had already repainted the little place, repaired the roof and the storage shed, fixed the fence, put in a chicken coop, and shoveled up the garden plot for some late squash, radishes, beans, and corn. The garden, a plot about forty feet square, extending down the gentle slope behind the house toward the creek, needed some weeding. Looking down past it and the sycamores, Bradley could see fish rising in the pond formed in the creek by a beaver dam. He hadn't been fishing yet, and if he had had some time this morning, it would have gone for garden work. But he didn't have time for either.

He started into town on foot, delaying his morning pipe in order to enjoy the scents along the way. Because this area south of the town abounded in small creeks and springs, in harsh contrast to the arid northern reaches of the canyon, trees of many varieties choked the narrow dirt road. Wild flowers were in bloom among the brush despite the heat and lack of rainfall. At the Jennings place, a small house along the road, the older residents were still sleeping; but the morning sun beamed through leafy tree openings onto a profusion of azaleas and rhododendrons.

Emerald Canyon's lush southern reaches, in contrast to its

parched northern arm, had given rise, perhaps, to the old Indian legends about the place. It was said that a young Indian warrior, hounded by enemies, had come here generations ago to hide. He had, the stories said, found a magic stone, an emerald which caused water to spring from the ground wherever he touched it. In his wanderings he had caused the springs and creeks of the southern area, while the northern portions remained as they had been for countless years earlier.

White men had finally driven the Indians from the canyon, which had been a holy place reserved for special hunting trips and ceremonials. But some of the legends remained. On a morning like this, with the smells of flowers and water and fresh greenery in his nostrils, Bradley could not help thinking about what the Indians had had here . . . wondering if the canyon had been taken from them with any shred of rightness or justice.

Reaching the edge of town, he found it gray and still under the slanting rays of the morning sun. The air was cool and the sky already a brilliant blue which would shade toward yellow, and then a fierce bronze, as the heat came with the passing hours.

He walked to the scene of the fire.

The storage shed had been little more than a ruin before the fire. Now nothing was left but some mounded black ash and scorched brush. Some thirty or forty yards away, other storage sheds, lean-tos, and abandoned sod structures lined up along the street. But this shed had been by itself, empty, and yet it had been the one to catch fire.

Bradley walked around the site, kicking idly at the black wreckage. The sharp odors of burned wood rose around him.

Squatting in the center of the charred ruin, he poked about with his hands. Some of the heavier beams were still warm underneath. He pulled a couple of long pieces out from underneath and tossed them to one side, then scooped soggy ashes and dirt over them to make sure they did not burst into new flames. Ash and dirt stuck to his hands and arms and face as he waded back into the middle of the small pile, dug around a little more, and almost got ready to give up.

Then his fingers uncovered something grayish white. He tugged at it. A piece of rag pulled grudgingly out of the bottom of the pile, and with it came some more rags, these charred badly.

Bradley raised one of the rags to his face and sniffed it. He felt a little prickle of realization.

He walked around a few more minutes, but found nothing more.

Taking the walk around the edge of town, he intersected the county road and proceeded to the old buffalo wallow. He examined the dusty roadway, but there were too many footprints to make out any sign. Moving with care, he returned to the beaten-down place in the grass where his attacker had lain in wait for him. He examined the area slowly, moved about in the grass all around it, walked to the wallow, and inspected its circumference.

The sun moved higher in the sky, beating warm against his back. He had a headache, and his weak leg bothered him a little. Although he moved efficiently, he did not hurry. It was after eight o'clock when he walked back to Main Street.

Two large old wagons were pulled up in the middle of the street near Jean Reff's café. Boards had been used to build up the sides of the wagons and they were packed high with corn, many of the shucks already quite yellow with age. The dray horses stood docile, flies buzzing around them. The drivers were not in view.

Bradley started toward the café. A thick-set man, wearing a wide straw hat and battered bib overalls, appeared in the doorway. Although he was middle-aged, and one of his shirt sleeves was pinned up, betraying a missing arm, he radiated robust potency.

"Jim!" he called softly in greeting.

Bradley grinned as he walked to the café door to meet Phil Schmitz. "You're out early enough, Phil."

"*Ja*," Schmitz grunted with satisfaction. "It is a long trip all the way to Ferndale, eh?"

They went into the café. Three of the other co-operative farmers were perched on stools at the counter, and Jean Reff, looking a little sleepy-eyed but just as pretty, was serving huge breakfasts. The coffee smelled good and everyone was in high spirits.

Bradley straddled a stool beside the other men. "This is about the last of the corn you'll move out, isn't it?"

"It is," Schmitz agreed, stabbing a fried egg with his fork. "Even this, it has gotten too old and will be for feeder use only. But in Ferndale we can sell it for good price."

Jean Reff brought coffee for Bradley. "Why so early?" she smiled.

"Look at all the interesting people I meet."

One of the other farmers, a man named Fain, put down his coffee cup for a refill. "Jim knows he has to be nice to us. After all, Phil is gonna be one of the new town board members."

"Ah," Schmitz growled, "you count chickens too fast. We got campaign ahead, plenty of work."

"You'll win," Jean said.

"We wait and see," Schmitz insisted, his big head bobbing for emphasis.

"The filing period is just around the corner," Bradley pointed out.

"And them board members is shaking in their boots already," Fain said.

"We got lots of work to do," Schmitz said. "John McCollum and me, we don't file for glory or *fun*. You think running for office fun? You don't understand this country. Be official, you must be good man. In democracy best man win election, lead other people. We got to convince citizens we are best, John and me."

"They're shaking in their boots," Fain repeated, and leaned forward to see Bradley. "You know how we pool our profits, and Phil and John put 'em in that rented safe in the bank? I'll tell you what: Nobody knows exactly how much cash we've got in there right now. The bank don't know since we've got the only keys. It's driving them crazy. I heard somebody say the other day we've got enough money in there to make sure we contact everybody in the canyon and promise 'em a chicken if they vote for us."

The other men laughed. Two months ago they had been individuals, powerless, on the brink of bankruptcy and foreclosure. Formation of the co-operative had given them means to haul water, and to get their goods hauled to a distant market where prices could not be manipulated. Now, with Schmitz and John McCollum acting as their officers, they were actually banking money—putting it into a rented vault which the bank could not examine. Their laughter reflected the heady sensation of prosperity—and confidence—after desperation.

"We are not so rich," Schmitz said, however. "Remember, almost all of us got payment to Strider Land Company later this week. Tomorrow, maybe day after, John and me, we got to come in, fix up ledger book, draw out money for every man to pay."

"We'll still have money left for what we need," Fain argued.

"Maybe so," Schmitz grunted. "We look at ledger and see. Everything is in ledger."

One of the others grinned. "We know that. You think we don't trust you?"

"You don't have to trust," Schmitz said. "It is all in ledger."

"If we didn't trust people like you and the marshal, here," Fain said, "I don't know who we could trust."

"Maybe try trust in God, little bit," Schmitz muttered.

One of the men finished eating and turned on his stool. He squinted at the bright sunlight beyond the windows. "Well, it's a good day for hauling, anyway."

"When do you come back?" Bradley asked.

"Tomorrow."

"Well, I'll make it a point to ride out past your places late today to make sure everything is all right."

"Some of our men will do that," Schmitz said.

"I know how well you're organized, Phil. But it's part of my job."

"Look like you got plenty job in town last night, eh?"

"You heard about that?"

"Everybody hear. Big excitement."

"I'm surprised," Bradley admitted, "that the news got out your way so fast."

"John McCollum and me, we was in town last night."

Bradley was surprised. "I didn't see you."

"*Ja*, we were here. Henry Strider ask us to come in, talk about how and when we will pay the land payments due. We talk at his office, just us two, him." Schmitz smiled with grim satisfaction. "We tell him, we pay lump sum, late tomorrow, next day. Out of vault. I think he hope we can't pay."

"We can pay." Fain grinned.

"You should have come by to say hello," Bradley said.

"You had plenty business without us, brother!"

"That's true."

"You catch somebody?"

"No."

"The break-in, the fire. They connect, you think?"

So they did not know about the shooting. "I doubt it," Bradley lied.

"Maybe accident," Schmitz said.

"Maybe. Right."

Fain said, "Let's get onto that road."

Schmitz sighed, drained his coffee cup, refused Jean's offer of a refill, and put some coins on the top of the counter. "Good as usual, lady."

"You're always welcome."

The men got down from the stools.

"I'll watch you pull out," Bradley said, joining them.

"You ain't had your breakfast," Schmitz said. "A man needs to eat, keep his strength up."

"I'll walk out with you," Bradley said easily.

Outside, the men checked the loading of the wagons and Bradley had a moment off to the side with the old German farmer.

"Phil, have you seen any strangers out your way?" he asked.

Schmitz scowled and thought for a moment. "No. Why do you ask?"

"Well, with the break-in last night, I'm just checking things."

"You walk out here to make sure the woman don't know you are worried?"

"I'm not worried," Bradley lied.

"Ha," Schmitz grunted. "But that is all right, Jim. You want to protect her from knowing you worried, that is good. Man treats his woman that way."

"She's not my woman."

Schmitz looked at him.

"She's not," Bradley insisted.

The wagons creaked as the men climbed around to the front seats. "Ready, Phil!" one of them called.

Schmitz clapped a hand on Bradley's shoulder. "We talk another time, eh?"

"Have a good trip."

Schmitz climbed ponderously to the platform of the front wagon, untied the reins, eased off the foot brake, and clucked at the team. The big horses leaned into the harness and the wagons groaned into movement.

Bradley stepped back, watching them go. It was good, seeing them roll. The co-operative was good for all of them, made this possible.

He was also aware, however, of the lurking worry. He had the intuition that last night's events had not been as random as they might appear. He had precious little to go on in trying to check this feeling out. The shotgun shell casings were common enough, offered no lead. And no one knew about that except himself and the unknown attacker.

He did not intend to tell anyone, either. He would also keep it to himself about the rags he had found at the bottom of the fire rubble. It would not serve anybody's interest for word to spread that the marshal had found rags, soaked in kerosene, at the site of the fire in a supposedly abandoned, empty storage shed.

He turned and went back toward the café, putting on his relaxed expression.

The front door of the sod-covered dugout was open, allowing sunlight to flood into the dark but immaculate interior. Gathering up the dishes from the table, John McCollum placed them in the washing basin and turned to the bedstead in the corner where his wife lay. "Any more coffee?" he asked cheerfully.

Mary McCollum smiled lazily, her hands at rest over the mound of her abdomen under the covers. "I'm fine. I'm going to get up now."

"Stay where you are," McCollum told her. "Dr. Ogleby said to stay in bed most of every day."

"I was in bed *all* day yesterday, dear. That means I can get up today and do a little housework—"

"Don't be silly, Mary!"

"The total time for the two days will balance out."

"You're being ridiculous," McCollum told her gently, "and you know it. You have to take it easy both for your own sake and for the baby's."

"The baby is fine. Do you want to feel him kick?"

"It isn't just the baby, either. You know you still have a lot of healing to do."

His wife sighed and readjusted her position in the bed. "All right, but I'm going to pout all day. You might as well know that."

"Good. I'll go outside and work, where I won't have to watch you."

"You're a very bad person, John McCollum."

"I know."

"Come over here and feel the baby."

He sat on the edge of the bed. He put his flat hand on her stomach. The child inside her kicked strongly.

"See?" she breathed. "We're both just *fine*."

McCollum did not reply. The miracle of life was too awesome to joke about. For them it was even more, because of Mary's injury.

Two months earlier, during the worst time surrounding controversy about formation of the farmers' co-operative, men had come to the farm to tear things up. Mary McCollum was not supposed to be there, but she was. She had been shot, and for a time her life—and then use of her legs—had been in the balance.

Dr. Ogleby said she was far on the road to full recovery now, and use of her legs had come back swiftly. The baby clearly was viable and strong. She could carry their son or daughter to full term now, safely. If she took it easy as the doctor ordered.

"So you see how strong we both are," she told McCollum now. "So I'll just get up."

"No."

"Why?"

"You know why."

"I'll be careful."

"No."

"Drat."

McCollum winked at her and got to his feet. He walked to the door that led out and up to ground level. "I'll check back on you in a little while, and I'd better find you resting."

She glared with make-believe spite. "Yes, O lord and master."

Chuckling, he climbed the three steps out of the sod-covered dugout. The sky was clear and it was already hot, with a light north wind. The area around the house had few trees, and in three directions there was little but rolling grassland and pasture to relieve the monotony. In the far distance was the high rim of the canyon. Behind the house, and slightly off to one side, there was a gentle depression in the earth. Some brush and a few small trees clung to life there. McCollum's tool shed stood at the far end of the garden plot under some of these small trees, and downslope to the gully were more of them. He had had a few cows down in the gully and trees before the marauders had come and killed them on that same day when Mary was injured.

Walking to the tool shed, however, McCollum reminded himself that he should have no time or place in his life for regrets. The attack on Mary and his property had solidified the farmers of the northern part of the canyon—once derisively called Yanks by more fortunate people at the far end of the canyon—and had made the co-op work. Personally, he had been blessed not only with Mary's recovery, but by saving of the child. And by hard work he had even gotten some of his garden back into shape.

Reaching the shed, he reached up to pull the metal pin from the lock hasp. Surprisingly, the pin hung along the jamb on its cord. McCollum frowned. He always latched the door, but did not lock it, against the unpredictable wind. A night storm could bang a door open and break the hinges if it were allowed to flap. He *always* put the pin in the hasp.

Opening the door, he peered into the shed. His tools, the bag of feed, and the sacks and cans of seeds were undisturbed. Everything was normal, which meant that certainly no one had entered to steal something.

Maybe he had just forgotten to slip the pin into place yesterday.

Getting out his hoe and mattock, he dismissed the momentary puzzle from his mind. He walked into the garden and started down a row of late peanuts, lightly breaking the ground around them and pulling out some weeds. There was talk about members of the co-operative trying to grow peanuts on a large scale next year, for shipment to the East. A few of them were going to try cotton in the spring, too. Working together they could try many things that no individual owned enough land to do well.

The co-operative was still viewed as a dangerous thing in some quarters. McCollum knew there were many in the canyon itself who viewed it as even sinister, a kind of un-American alliance, for farmers to band together this way. In the first flush of reaction against the violence that had broken out two months ago over water hauling rights, nearly everyone had sided with the farmers, and with Marshal Jim Bradley. But since that time there had been nothing to rally support, and McCollum knew that old doubts had begun to crop up again. Farmers were supposed to be *individuals,* some said, and there was something intrinsically wrong—and threatening—when they worked together as members of the co-operative did.

Still, the co-operative had changed the members' lives. Together they could haul water. Together they could ship produce out of the canyon to better and needier markets that offered better prices. Money was being banked; land payments could be made on schedule. There would be no foreclosures this fall.

McCollum wondered how Phil Schmitz, his fellow co-op officer, was doing on the trip outside with the corn. Tomorrow, if things went well, Schmitz would be back. The next day they would go to the bank and get the cash money from the box to make the farm payments. After that, they would rebalance the books and hold a meeting to tell all members where they stood. McCollum knew there were going to be some happy faces at *that* meeting. The co-operative was going to have more than two thousand dollars left after making all the payments and meeting its other obligations.

That meant water wells which could be drilled during the

winter. It meant new change, new improvements, for all of them. In another year, with luck, each family would have a nice individual bonus. Houses could be fixed up. New clothes could be purchased. Everything would be on the mend at an even faster clip.

Hoeing, McCollum marveled again at how he had come to be cochairman of the co-op. He did not feel very worthy, but it was a responsibility he would not shirk. It was a real honor. For the co-op, like life in Emerald Canyon, had become the basis of his commitment.

He continued to work steadily. The sun beat on his back and the sweat came.

At a little after nine o'clock, H. R. Yeager came into Jim Bradley's jail office in a high state of agitation. The bulky, gray-haired man was in his shirt sleeves, and he had even forgotten to remove the green eyeshade he usually wore while working on books at his savings company, which most people referred to as a bank.

"Jim," he said grimly, "you'd better get right down there with me."

Bradley moved from his rolltop desk. "What's happened?"

"I think there was a break-in last night."

Asking no more questions immediately, Bradley grabbed his hat and went with him.

"I can't tell anything has been bothered," Yeager muttered as they hurried down the plank sidewalk on the shady side.

"How do you know somebody broke in?"

"I *don't* know, for certain. But the side window has been pulled out of the frame. I think someone broke in, then tried to hide it by putting the window back in place as well as they could."

"When did you find it?"

"A few minutes ago, when I went into the side office where the window is located."

They reached the small building. Of frame construction, it

was one of the sturdiest along the street and in a good state of repair. The lock on the front door, which Yeager now opened with a key, was sturdy, too.

"I sent Mrs. Bryce to the café for some breakfast," Yeager explained, swinging the door open. "She doesn't know. No need to get word out about this."

"Who else does know?" Bradley asked, stepping into the large, dusty front room.

"Nobody."

Yeager led the way to the side office. It contained only a desk and chair and bookcase, empty. He pointed mutely to the window.

Bradley's examination confirmed what Yeager had said. The window had been pried loose from outside, then lifted out. He found crowbar marks indented deeply into the soft wood of the frame on the outside, and there were numerous splinters and small wood chunks in the dirt of the little walking space between buildings. It looked as Yeager had said: someone had removed the window, then replaced it with some care, even banging home a few bright new nails as if they hoped no one would notice.

"You're sure this happened last night?" Bradley asked, back in the office.

"Yes."

"It couldn't have happened earlier, and you just noticed today?"

"I washed the windows the day before yesterday. It wasn't like that then."

"Could it have happened the night before last?"

Yeager frowned. "I don't think so. Look here, Jim. There was other commotion last night. Isn't it logical to believe this was a part of it? Maybe the *main* part?"

"I was thinking the same thing," Bradley admitted. "But if the object of the confusion was to break in here, what's missing?"

"I've looked. Like I told you: nothing."

"You're sure of that?"

"I couldn't be surer."

"Let's check again."

Yeager shrugged. "All right. You can see nothing in this room has been disturbed. Nothing to disturb anyway." He led the way out into the main office, with its desks and counter. "Supplies are under the shelving, there. All in fine shape. Desks haven't been disturbed." Walking around the back desk, he took a key off a ring and opened a wood door. "The vaults are in here, of course. Come in."

Bradley followed him. In the smaller inside room, which had no windows and no other doors, one wall was dominated by racks on which rested small metal lockboxes. They were lined up neatly, locks in place. Across the room, in the inside corner, stood a very large steel safe, its combination-lock door securely closed. Beside it stood a smaller safe with a key lock on its heavy door.

"I checked the main vault," Yeager said. "Everything in good order."

"How about the smaller one?"

"That's the one the farmers are renting."

"Did you open it?"

"There are only two keys in the world to that small safe, Jim. Phil Schmitz has one and John McCollum has the other."

"It's all right, then, too," Bradley decided. "What about your own office?"

Yeager led the way. His office contained several big filing cabinets of documents and loan papers, but they were still locked from overnight, and a quick check showed nothing out of order.

Finally the two men walked back to the main reception room.

"The only thing I can figure," Bradley said, "is that someone started to break in, got spooked, and ran away before they could do anything."

"If that's so, why did they take time to renail the window?"

"That," Bradley admitted disgustedly, "is a puzzle."

"Well," Yeager sighed, "I'm going to go look up old Charlie. He used to sleep here after he did his clean-up chores, you know. I think I'll just ask him to resume that practice."

"Not a bad idea. And I'll make it a point to walk all the way around on my rounds, and let you or Charlie know if there's anything at all out of the ordinary."

"They might try again."

Bradley scratched his chin and thought about it.

"Jim."

"Yes?"

"For the sake of the business . . . not a word about this, all right?"

"I understand," Bradley said. "I'll make a brief report for my file, but I won't say a word to anyone."

"It would be very bad if this got out. Shake public confidence. A savings institution such as this one has to have public confidence above all things."

Bradley thought about some of the incredible interest rates Yeager charged to the down-and-out. How, he wondered, did those loans build public confidence?

Perhaps, he thought, it was not his business. At least—again—there had been only a near-miss, and not a major crime. He could not quite decide whether his luck was suddenly running much better or much worse. After a few more minutes of conversation with Yeager, he walked back to his office to worry some more.

FOUR

Friday morning was cloudy. John McCollum sat astride his old mare, Molly, at the dirt crossroads south of his house and watched the clouds move in, thickening. The wind was steady and humid, promising rain. It was due, McCollum thought.

After he had waited a few minutes, he saw another horseman coming up the narrow east road. He was able to recognize the man he was awaiting, Phil Schmitz, at a considerable distance. Schmitz's bulk gave him away, and a one-armed man, somehow, sat his horse a little differently. McCollum supposed it was a matter of balance.

While he waited for Schmitz to close the gap and join him, McCollum reflected briefly on the circumstances that had made them friends as well as co-leaders of the farmers' co-operative. Schmitz's leadership role was natural, as one of the oldest "Yank" farmers and a man universally liked; he had come to Emerald Canyon four years ago with his large brood of strapping youngsters and a robust, always smiling wife, and perhaps he would have been able to cling to an existence even without the co-op; he had lasted longer than most before its inception.

McCollum's role was different. He was among the newest residents. Only the previous spring he had brought his bride here, lured by the offer of cheap farmland "in an area of great abundance" with easy payments spaced to coincide with crop harvests. McCollum, like so many who had come and failed before him, had not had the money to investigate—had come with only his small wagonload of possessions and enough money to make a down payment and buy a few essentials. Without luck and the rise of the co-op, he would have been ruined by now.

There was nothing illegal in the land maneuvering that had taken place here for a long time. No one was forced to buy land, and the prices were reasonable enough. When the rains came, a man could eke out a living. When the rain refused to come, then it was legitimate for Strider Land Company to foreclose, give back none of the money that had already been paid, and sell the land to some new unwitting victim.

McCollum knew that men like Henry Strider and others who had long held power here could not like the co-op or the changes it was making. And yet there had been little real hostility. Jim Bradley had something to do with that, as did public opinion. As a matter of fact, the co-op and its improvements had begun with gentle stirrings of fragile public opinion, and remained in existence because of them. It was a delicate balance and the co-op had to move cautiously and reasonably in offering goods for the best prices, trying to maneuver deliveries to take advantage of market conditions, without arousing enmity locally.

Schmitz, McCollum thought, was ideal for this job. The wily German knew his business and he knew people. He was honest and a natural leader. But McCollum's own role continued to surprise him. He wondered if he had become a co-leader only because the water hauling for irrigation had been his idea and his plan—that and the fact that the attack on Mary had created public sympathy. He did not feel easy about his responsibility, at any rate.

Schmitz rode up and joined him. The older man had a fat ledger book stuck in the front of his bib overalls.

"Sorry I am late, John!"

"I was early."

"Some creature got into our barn. Possibly a raccoon. I

found tools overturned, eh? And some hay knocked out of the loft. So I looked for the varmint."

"You didn't find him?"

Schmitz sighed. "*Ach,* no. But no harm was done, so it is all right. I mention it only to tell you why I am late."

They turned their horses toward town.

"We have lots of time," McCollum observed.

Schmitz patted the ledger book. "It will be pleasure, yes? Giving Henry Strider his payments?"

"It will," McCollum agreed. "Your trip to market went fine, too?"

"*Ja.* We came back late last night. We did good. The corn was needed there for feed. We get good price. I have the money here." He patted his pocket.

"Do you have the exact figure in the ledger book on how much we have to withdraw for the members' payments?"

"I do. I worked on it last night. I did hard work on the figures. The news is all good, John."

"My payment is more than two hundred dollars." McCollum did not try to hide his touch of worry.

"That is average," Schmitz said. "But we can cover all that. Every member—all forty-one of us—will be paid."

"A lot of money."

"Eight thousand, six hundred and some dollars."

Despite knowing that the figure would be high, McCollum flinched.

"Is all right." Schmitz smiled. "I have done arithmetic. You know how much we will have in vault when we add this money I have in pocket?"

"I know it's a good amount."

Schmitz pulled a slip of paper from his shirt pocket. "I wrote down. Look."

McCollum took the slip of paper and read the penciled total. It startled him. The figures read: *$11,746.28.*

"We *definitely* can start some wells, then!"

"*Ja.*"

"And we'll have some left over—for clothes. I know we *hoped*, but—"

"*Ja!* And hopes coming true!"

McCollum thought about it and shook his head in bewilderment. "All this money. Alone, we were so poor."

"We will all make our own way now, eh?"

McCollum grinned. "I can't wait to get there and let Henry Strider see the color of our money."

Schmitz touched his heels against the flanks of his horse. "Come, then! We hurry!"

They rode into town. Nothing much was going on. As an agricultural community with no large cattle spreads to lure rowdy drovers, Emerald Canyon seldom seemed to have much of an unusual nature going on. A few wagons were parked along the commercial row, the general stores, feed lots, clothing merchandisers, post office, shoe store, café. Some small children played in the street near the opera house, which had been shut down for over a year now. The clouds and threat of rain had perhaps brought some people to town ahead of their afternoon schedules, but the town would have been hard pressed to mount a traffic jam at any time.

Schmitz and McCollum rode to the Yeager savings and loan office, dismounted, tied their horses, walked inside. H. R. Yeager and his assistant were at work at desks behind the counter. Yeager looked up, blinked, and came to greet them. "Good morning, gentlemen!"

"We come for use of safe," Schmitz said.

"Fine! Fine!" Yeager walked back to his desk, got a key ring from the top drawer, and led the way to the door which led into the vault area. He made a commotion out of unlocking the door, and went in first. "Here we are."

"Good," Schmitz said, frowning down at the small safe which they rented. "We thank you, Mr. Yeager."

"If you need help—"

"No. Thank you."

Yeager hesitated. He did not like it, McCollum thought, the way they forced him to leave the room, granting them their privacy. But then H. R. Yeager was certainly not the only person around who wondered just how much money their work had allowed them to salt away.

It was going to be grand to show them.

After a moment, Yeager walked out of the room.

Schmitz winked at McCollum, fished his key out of his shirt, where it hung on a chain, put the ledger book and a wad of money on top of the safe, and knelt to open the door.

The lock was slightly tricky, and usually required some fiddling with the key in the slot. This time, however, it turned readily. With a soft exclamation of pleasure, Schmitz pulled the door open.

"Gott!" he cried, staring into the safe.

"What?" McCollum said, alarmed.

Schmitz sank backward in a curiously comical slow motion, his weight going off his feet as he fell back, actually, onto his buttocks. He continued to stare. His eyes bulged terribly and his mouth gaped. As he tried to speak, only a guttural mouthing of noise came from him. He pointed at the interior of the steel box, tried again to speak, failed.

Beginning to suspect the one thing, the worst thing—the only thing bad enough to make Phil Schmitz react this way—McCollum took a step forward and bent over to look into the safe. He was already terrified of what he might see, although the suspicion was impossible.

But correct.

The safe was empty.

The bunkhouse downslope from Samuel Kane's big house, screened from its view by trees, was quiet. The ranch hands were away from the house area, some checking and moving cattle, others cleaning out a field barn two miles away, still others working on a bad spot in the road that led here from town. The long, narrow, low-roofed shed where these men slept and kept their meager possessions was now occupied by only three persons: Kane himself, Paul Lars, and the man they called Bing.

Uneasy because of the way the meeting had been sought, Kane hid the concern and faced his two hired men with hard seriousness. "Now, what's this about?"

Despite the air of tension, Bing showed nothing. Painfully slender, of medium height, he peered solemnly at Kane from under the brim of his big Stetson. The foreman was not a true albino, for his eyes were a magical green. But his skin never tanned and he was always careful to wear a hat and long sleeves in even the fiercest heat, saying the sun burned him too readily. He had milky skin, white hair, and silvery eyebrows. He might have been taken for a weakling if it were not for his eyes, his manner, and his hidden background which only Kane knew for a certainty.

"Like I told you," Bing said in that deceptive, almost womanlike tone. "Paul, here, is tense."

"Tense?" Kane repeated the odd word. "What does that mean, Lars?"

Paul Lars was Bing's opposite: squat, swarthy, roughly dressed, a man whose checkered past and angry disposition showed out of every pore. His cheek was distended by tobacco when he spoke. "I told Bing."

"Suppose you tell me."

Lars's eyes were furtive. "I think I got more money coming."

"More money?"

"That's the short of it."

Kane controlled himself. "Why should you have more money coming, Lars?"

Lars looked around the room as if haunted.

"You can talk," Kane prodded him. "There's no one else around."

Lars shifted his cud of tobacco to the other cheek. "That job I did the other night."

"What about it?"

"I took a lot of risks. It was a hard job. I could have been *caught.*"

So that was it. Kane had guessed it earlier but now it was confirmed. He decided, however, to have it in the open. "You knew it was risky, Lars. You had an option. It was not required."

"I know," Lars said, with a quick glance toward Bing. "But I been thinking." He paused, his throat worked, and then he spat it out. "A hundred dollars just ain't enough."

"Three months' pay isn't enough for a few hours' work?"

"Look at the chances I took! Breakin' that door! Settin' the fire and makin' that ruction at the park! Then them kids came along and I almost didn't get away after the shot I taken at Bradley!"

"But you did get away with it," Kane pointed out, his eyes meeting Bing's momentarily. "You followed orders and it went just as we said it would. You have no complaint."

Lars's face glistened with sweat now, but he shook his head stubbornly. "A hundred ain't enough."

"When you were hired, it was agreed you wouldn't be asked about your past. You've worked just like the other men. We agreed there might be . . . extra chores, from time to time. Confidential assignments. In the time you've been here, you've been given four such assignments. This one paid better than the others."

"I know, but—"

"You have a chance," Kane went on coldly, "to do even better in the future. I reward men who are loyal, and do good work. But you disappoint me, Lars. This is no way to treat an employer who has lived up to his end of the bargain."

Lars shook his head. "I just think I ought to get more. The risk—"

"*I* think you've been adequately paid," Kane said, beginning to lose his temper.

Lars stared at him. The man's broad face became sullen. "I got more coming. I see what's going on here, some."

Kane chilled. "What does that mean?"

"I mean you've got a lot at stake. I mean there are folks who would pay a lot to know what I done—who told me to do it."

"You wouldn't tell them, though, would you, Lars?"

Lars stared at him, startled by the silken tone.

"I mean," Kane said, "you're loyal. Isn't that right?"

"I'm loyal, yeah. I've got more money coming. That's all I got in mind. I just want you to know—"

"That you feel you've been shortchanged? A friendly reminder?"

"That's right." Lars seemed to relax slightly. "Yeah. I ain't trying to hold anybody up or anything. I just want you to know how I feel about it, is all."

Kane felt a certain hidden sadness. "All right, Lars. I understand your position."

"I feel like another fifty would be right," Lars said hopefully.

"I'm going to have to think about this," Kane told him. "I can see the logic behind what you're saying. I suppose, thinking about it now, you're right. You did do a hard night's work, and took risks."

"That's true," Lars said, brightening. "I ain't out to hold anybody—"

"Yes. You said that, and I understand. But I have to ponder the matter, too. You understand that?"

"Sure," the man said, his expression showing that he didn't.

"I have to manufacture some trip for you to make, you understand, so the extra money will be a bonus for that, rather than just coming out of the blue. That will require some thinking, too."

"Yeah," Lars said more hopefully still. "I getcha."

"I appreciate you being out in the open with this," Kane told the man. "It helps all of us to be honest. We have a good working relationship, and that has to be based on honesty all around. Let me think about this, and I'll try to have word for you by tomorrow."

"Good," Lars said. "I appreciate it, Mr. Kane. You know, it ain't easy, askin' for more money, but—"

"I understand," Kane said. And he smiled. "Let me suggest you get yourself on down to the field barn. Put in a good day's work. Bing and I will get our heads together here and work out some sort of trip for you that ought to make an extra bonus look legitimate."

"Right." Lars lumbered toward the door, then turned back. "There's nothing personal in this, Mr. Kane. You're a fair boss. You've treated me good. I just thought you ought to know—"

"I thank you for it, too, Lars. No harm done. We're all better for getting it on the table."

Lars nodded, glanced at the silent Bing, then went outside. The screen door banged behind him.

"Well, Bing," Kane said, "I think Lars has a point. We don't want a man to take too much risk for the payment we offer. The cost of everything is sky-high these days, and he did risk capture, especially the way he was interrupted outside of town with the marshal."

As Kane spoke, Bing moved with fluid grace to the side window. He peered outside past the wood slats.

"Therefore," Kane went on, "I believe some additional errand should be trumped up, and then we can give Lars the proper—"

"It's all right," Bing said quietly.

"He's gone?"

"Walked down to the corral. I can see him saddling his horse."

Kane got a cigar from his coat pocket and bit off the end, spitting it violently into the corner. "He's a greedy man, Bing. He's also regrettably stupid."

Bing stared at Kane from the shadow of his hat and shelf of white eyebrows. He did not reply.

"We can't have a man thinking about going to the marshal, or anyone else, for that matter," Kane said.

Bing rested his hand lightly on the butt of the Colt's revolver on his right hip. His strange eyes remained on Kane's face. Even Kane, man that he was, felt a deep chill.

"The trouble, of course," Kane went on, "is that a man is never any good anymore once he gets into the habit of making extra demands . . . throwing threats around. He *becomes* a threat."

Bing watched him without a sound.

"We can't have threats," Kane added.

Bing took a deep breath and started toward the door, moving like a panther, only his chunking spurs making a sound. He reached the door and turned back. "I don't think you got to worry, Mr. Kane," he said gently.

"Good," Kane said.

Bing turned and went out, the door whispering behind him.

Kane went to the window and watched his foreman walk easily, with that economical gait of his, down to the corral. He joined Lars there, and also began saddling a horse. Kane saw Lars's penetrating glance at the pale gunman, as if Lars were trying to make sure of his intentions.

Poor Lars.

He was not a stupid man, really, Kane thought. He was, in fact, much cleverer than most, and good at his highly specialized kind of work. But he could not know how far over his head he was in trying to outthink or outwit a man like Bing.

Kane had researched the backgrounds of a number of men before finally hiring Bing. There was none better.

Bing was thirty-two. Originally from Kentucky, he had left that state at the age of sixteen after killing a fellow youth in an argument over a girl. Later, under another name, he had worked and lived for a time in Chicago, and Kane's information was that he had been near the center of the famous robbery that struck an Atchison, Topeka & Santa Fe train in

1861, a robbery in which fourteen soldiers were killed and an undisclosed sum in pure gold had vanished.

According to Kane's information, Bing had been double-crossed following the robbery. Authorities were puzzled to this day about the series of bizarre murders that had struck some of the proven participants in the two years following the robbery, but Kane thought he knew who had done the killings, and why.

Avoiding service in the Civil War, at least as far as uniformed combat was involved, Bing had next appeared in or near Sedalia in the late sixties. It was whispered that he worked for anyone who could pay his price, and that his tools were his gun and knife. On the surface he was a professional meat hunter. Those who knew better were either men who needed his services, and were not likely to talk, or those on whom he performed his work, and were in no shape to talk to anyone again, ever.

In 1870 Kane had been looking for a new general foreman and had heard that Bing, under still another name, was in the Kansas prison. The whole business had been very tricky, but Kane had been able to verify this, and finally use influence to get Bing out. Since that time Bing had worked for him. Kane paid him a very, very high wage. Bing could do ordinary work, and do it well, and he was good with the men. Some suspected his past and feared him, while others, if they did so, hid it well. Certainly there was no trouble.

A man in power, Kane had long ago decided, needed at least one strong right hand on whom he could always depend, in any circumstances: a man upon whom he could call for *whatever* needed to be done.

He had not been forced to call on Bing's special talents often, but he knew those talents were untarnished by the passage of time. He knew about Bing's frequent brief absences, and knew where he secreted himself for practice with his guns or the terrible drinking bouts that often followed this compulsive practice.

There were things in this man's past, Kane thought now, that no other man could ever fathom. The terrible constant practice, the deceptive calm, the brutal past, the periodic drinking which no one ever knew about—they spoke of a man who was complex and driven, perhaps bitterly unhappy and perhaps even not entirely sane.

But he was loyal, Bing was, and Kane could take comfort now from knowing that Bing would handle the Paul Lars problem. Oh yes. Bing was always there if something like this came along. Bing had never failed, and never would. He was, perhaps, even the ultimate weapon against Jim Bradley . . . if all else failed, although Kane did not like to think about this possibility because Bradley was good, too, and popular, and although Kane knew Bing would win in a confrontation, he might also be destroyed in the process.

With a man like Paul Lars, however, it would not be so difficult. It would be . . . taken care of. There would be no mess. Not any mess that anyone ever found.

Thinking about it, Kane had an uncharacteristic momentary chill. This happened sometimes when he thought too deeply about the potential of this man he called his own, this man named Bing.

"It is gone!"

"I can *see* it's gone, Schmitz. That's not my fault!"

"You said the safe was trustworthy!"

"You and McCollum have the only keys in the world for the thing."

"*Ach!* You are saying we *took our own money?*"

"I'm not saying anything."

Standing beside the obviously rifled safe, Jim Bradley held out his hands to try to calm them down. "Take it easy, gents."

Phil Schmitz turned bulging eyes toward him. "Where is our money?"

"I don't know, obviously. Let's try to get it straightened out."

Kneeling on the floor in front of the smaller safe, John McCollum stared at the open door and vacant interior. He seemed in shock. "It can't be," he muttered.

Bradley turned to Yeager, whose angry countenance betrayed the shock that he, too, had to be feeling. "You say there are no other keys to this box?"

"None! Just two! That's all there ever were, and these gentlemen demanded to have both of them."

"But the safe has not been broken!" Schmitz said. "A key must have been used, eh?"

"If so," Yeager growled, "it was one of your keys."

"Do you both have your keys?" Bradley demanded.

Schmitz, scowling, held out a hand with his key in it. McCollum nodded, dug into his pocket, and produced the companion key.

"Could either of you have misplaced the key long enough for someone to duplicate it?" Bradley asked.

"I don't see how," McCollum said. "I keep mine hidden in the—I keep mine well hidden. And Phil wears his on a chain around his neck."

"There was another key," Schmitz said, glaring at Yeager.

"No!" Yeager bellowed back.

"Wait a minute, now," Bradley intervened. "Let's try to get this all straight."

The three men looked at him and waited with expressions that said they might have some hope he could do just that— which was more than he was sure about.

"You came into town a little while ago," he said slowly. "You came here."

"Yes," McCollum said.

"You opened the safe and found it just like this?"

"That's right."

"When was the last time you were here to open the safe?"

"About three weeks ago."

Bradley glanced at Schmitz for corroboration and got it. "All the money was here at that time?"

"All," Schmitz said.

Bradley knelt to examine the safe. He could not find any sign of damage, not even a scratch or fresh damage to the faded black paint anywhere. The floor, back, sides, and top were heavy steel and were intact. There was no sign of tampering with the door or lock mechanism. He closed the door, turned the lock handle, and tried to force it open again with pressure on the handle. It was solid and wouldn't budge. When he borrowed McCollum's key, the door opened readily, the lock feeling solid as it turned inside the heavy door.

Bradley handed the key back. "Let's talk about the chance someone got one of these keys and duplicated it."

"It can't have happened, Jim," McCollum replied.

"You're sure?"

"As sure as I could be about anything. I don't want to say where I've had my key hidden, but if you want to come out to my place by yourself, I'll show you in secret. Nobody could find it. Nobody could get away with it long enough without my knowing the thing was missing."

Bradley turned to Schmitz.

The German touched the key on a chain around his thick neck. "Here is where it is. Always. It has not left this chain."

"Someone could have taken it during your sleep."

"I am light sleeper," Schmitz said with great dignity. "And I am not a fool, Jim, like maybe you think."

Bradley got slowly to his feet, regretting his question. Phil Schmitz and John McCollum were probably the best friends and strongest supporters he had in Emerald Canyon. Schmitz was quite within his rights to be angry at the foolish question: he was *not* a fool.

He was not a thief, either—any more than McCollum was.

"Let's talk about extra keys, Mr. Yeager," he said.

"I told you," Yeager said. "There aren't any extra keys. Never have been. Oh, let me tell you, I didn't like the idea of turning both keys over to these gentlemen. But they insisted. I finally said all right, it's your responsibility. They accepted that. Now we've had this ridiculous accident and you try to blame me."

"Calm down," Bradley said. "I'm not trying to blame anyone. I—"

"There are no other keys!"

"Then what do you think happened here?"

"I think one of their keys was taken. Someone got in here, opened the vault, took the money off."

"How could that happen, if you were watching the place as you're supposed to?"

"The burglary. We thought that window had been pried and then left. But what if someone got in?"

The idea had been at the edge of Bradley's mind and he had not wanted to let it in. Now he had to face it.

It was possible. They had assumed no one had gained entry because they had not been able to find any sign of anything missing. But now something very definitely *was* missing.

Yeager said, "Someone got one of these men's keys, made a copy, returned the original. Then that person created a commotion in town, and while everyone was running around with the fire and everything, he broke in here, quickly opened the vault, took the money, and got away before he was spotted."

"No one could have gotten a key, I tell you!" McCollum said.

"There's no other explanation," Yeager countered, "unless one of you two took the money yourself."

"What is this you say about us?" Schmitz demanded.

"I'm not saying that's what happened. I'm just saying—"

"We would steal the money of our friends?"

"I don't say you did. I'm just saying it has to be either that, or the burglar."

"Then was burglar," Schmitz said.

The four men stood silent.

Bradley was trying to make the situation hold together in his mind. It appeared that Yeager's burglary theory was the best bet. He hated to think so because that meant there was precious little chance of finding the culprit. Was there an angle he was overlooking?

Thinking aloud, he said, "We'll keep this quiet for a little while. I assume I can count on your co-operation."

"How can we keep it quiet?" McCollum asked. "We're supposed to deliver the land payments to the Strider Land Company this morning."

"Can it be delayed?"

"No. You know Henry Strider."

Schmitz added, "Is not just our money, Jim. Is money of all farmers. This cannot be hidden. We must tell what has happened."

"You're right. Why don't the two of you go on over there and explain to Strider what's happened. Then you'd better come on over to the jail office. I'll need to get statements from both of you."

"It is terrible thing," Schmitz said. "All money of our friends, the co-operative. This can mean ruin of everything, everything!"

"There are some things we can check out," Bradley said, trying to be reassuring. "Go explain to Henry Strider and then come to my office."

"But we are responsible! We have lost the money of all our friends!"

Bradley tried to ignore the pain in the old German's eyes. "Go tell Strider," he repeated. "Then come to my office."

Dazed, Schmitz walked unevenly to the office door. He went out of view.

McCollum said softly, "No one could have gotten our keys, Jim."

"I'll see you in my office in a few minutes, John."

After the two men had gone, H. R. Yeager stood first on one foot, then the other, while Bradley repeated and intensified his examination of the safe, the wall behind it, the floor— everything.

"It had to be opened by key," Bradley admitted finally.

Yeager said nothing.

"So the burglary has to be the explanation."

"Ask Schmitz about his visit that he didn't mention," Yeager said.

Bradley turned sharply. "What?"

"Ask Schmitz about his visit last week."

"*What* visit last week? He said they hadn't been here for three weeks."

Yeager's face was slack. "I heard him."

"Are you saying Phil Schmitz was here a week ago? Who was with him?"

"It was just before closing time. And he was alone."

Something tugged painfully at Bradley's insides, a suspicion he did not want to face. He studied Yeager's expression. "Are you saying Schmitz just lied to me?"

"Yes."

"Why would he do that?"

"I don't know. Maybe you'd better ask him that question."

"Phil Schmitz and John McCollum are as honest as the day is long," Bradley said. "We both know that!"

Yeager's face betrayed anger. "My establishment has never been robbed or burgled. This *may* have been a clever burglar. But ask Schmitz about his visit. He came in here, closed the door. I assumed he wanted in the safe. Ask him the question you just asked *me:* Why did he lie about his last visit? And what was the purpose of that visit a week ago yesterday?"

FIVE

Schmitz and McCollum had a hang-dog look when they appeared at Jim Bradley's office thirty minutes later. The jail cells were empty at the moment and Bradley's deputy was off duty, so they had the long, barren room to themselves. Sounds of voices came distantly from the adjoining City Building, where some sort of minor court case was in session.

"What did Strider say?" Bradley demanded.

"He said it has to be paid on time," McCollum said.

"Did you explain?"

"He was shocked. He said he was shocked. His word. But he said business is business." Bitterness flattened McCollum's voice. "What else did you expect?"

"He wouldn't give you *any* leeway?"

"He said," Schmitz replied, "his company will do all in its power to help. But what does it matter if he gives us another thirty days? Or sixty? Or *any* amount of time? If this money is lost, we are all finished. The harvest is all but done. There is no more money." His face set. "There is no more hope."

"Well, maybe things aren't as bad as they look," Bradley said meaninglessly.

"Nobody could have gotten my key," McCollum said.

"Mine was always with me," Schmitz added.

"Where did you hide your key?" Bradley asked.

"In the house. I hollowed out a place in one of the roof beams. Then I made a piece to cover over the small hole. You have to stand on the chair in the corner, with a lantern, to have any chance of seeing the seam. It fits tight and it isn't even within ordinary reach. I did it while my wife was still in town at the doctor's, recuperating. I tell you, no one saw me make the hiding place and a man could spend days in that house—even if he knew it was in the house—and not find that tiny niche."

Bradley thought about it. McCollum was a man who could be trusted, a careful and truthful man who left nothing to chance if he could help it. Bradley believed him. He turned to Schmitz.

"My key has not left this chain on my neck," Schmitz said. "I told you so. It is truth."

"But somebody did get into your safe."

"There has to be a third key."

"Yeager says no."

"Then Yeager has to be lying."

"I'll talk to him again," Bradley said. "Maybe he forgot an old key."

"It has to be that," McCollum said. "We didn't lose our keys."

If this was true, as Bradley thought it probably was, then the possibility of a tie-in with the seeming burglary, fire, and other commotion was remote at best. He felt himself tempted to believe one of his friends had lost his key for a few crucial hours in a way not understood: if this had happened, then the burglary and other commotion began to make some sense, just as Yeager had suggested.

It was appealing because it did tend to make sense.

But it meant McCollum and Schmitz were fools. He could not believe this.

"I suppose you'll have to report to the co-op," he said.

"We will call meeting tonight," Schmitz said heavily. "By then maybe most will know anyway. Word spreads fast, when the news is bad like this."

"Incidentally, when did you say you were last at the bank?"

"Three weeks."

"You're sure of that?"

Schmitz stiffened. "We are sure. We went together. Why?"

"I just wanted to be sure," Bradley said.

McCollum said, "It was three weeks ago, Jim. We're both sure."

The talk went on for a while, but got nowhere. When the two men left, they showed their deep worry and depression. Bradley did not envy them their worry, their shock, or the ordeal of having to tell the other poor farmers of the north end of the canyon.

But something else worried him more. Yeager said Schmitz had been in the office a week ago. Schmitz denied this. Someone was lying. Who?

Riding with Lars through rough brush toward the place where they were to join the work crew, Bing watched very carefully for the precise time and place and positioning that would best suit his purposes. He allowed some time to pass while they got well away from the house area. Now they were in a ravine section about midway between the house and the place the other men were working. The sound of a gunshot would not carry to another person's ear in this area.

They had been riding along side by side in silence.

They walked their horses into a little gully where the trees allowed only mottled sunlight down onto the thinly washed pebbles of the stream at the bottom. It was quiet and cool-damp out of the sun, and Bing was ready.

He pulled on his reins suddenly with a great show of alarm. "What was that?" he asked sharply.

Paul Lars, his face slack with surprise, also reined up. "What? Where?"

Bing pointed. "There. On your side. A rattler."

Lars froze, holding his horse very still. "I don't see him."

Bing pulled out his gun. "I'll take care of it."

Lars waited trustingly, eyes searching the rocks for the snake.

Bing heeled the hammer of the Colt back and fired. The explosion was loud. The bullet crashed into Paul Lars's side, hurling him off the saddle and into the wet gravel with a shallow splash. He cried out as he hit, and his horse lunged ahead, kicking him and then going up the side of the gully and into the brush with considerable racket.

Lars twitched, rolled over face-down in the wet gravel, and did not move.

Bing sat very still, easily controlling his own animal's frightened responses. He watched Paul Lars's still form for a full minute. Then he punched out the spent shell from his Colt and replaced it with a fresh one, holstered the gun, made a cigarette, and lighted it.

He would go on to the work area and ask for Lars, express impatience that he hadn't arrived yet, and spend most of the day with the other men. Later he could come back here under cover of darkness and make a shallow grave. In the meantime, the men could assume that Lars had simply gone off to some other job, some other part of the country. Men did that. There would be no hullabaloo.

It had been easy, as usual.

Bing left Lars where he lay, and rode on.

After thinking it over awhile, Jim Bradley went back to the Yeager savings and loan office. He re-examined the window that had been jimmied earlier, looked at the small safe again, and thought about it some more. He was deeply worried.

The next stop was Strider Land Company.

Henry Strider, affecting a scowl of concern, escorted him into the inner office and closed the door for privacy. Plucking a piece of lint from the sleeve of his coat, Strider offered a cigar and then rested his elbows on the immaculate surface of his big desk. "I assume this is about the tragedy with the money, Jim?"

"That's right."

"It's a terrible thing. I'm shocked. I mean that sincerely. Can you tell me if you have any leads on getting any of the money back?"

"There are things to work on," Bradley lied. "What I need to know from you is how much money you had coming on this payment series and what you might be able to do for these people if I can't get the money back right away."

Strider frowned. "There are several thousand dollars involved, Jim. Of course I'm not in position to give you a precise total without some adding up of accounts. I don't know if that would be proper, giving you an exact total. It's those farmers' business, after all. But I can say it's a large sum. Yes. As to what the firm can do to help, you may be sure we will do everything possible. I already told Mr. Schmitz and McCollum that of course we won't make any immediate demands. That would be grossly unfair. Grossly. We'll give them all the time we possibly can, within reason. Thirty days, even sixty. We aren't unreasonable."

Bradley kept his face smooth. He had never really understood the ways of business. He told himself that Strider was really trying to help. "What happens if we can't locate the money in the allotted time?"

Strider sighed. "I hope that doesn't happen, Jim, and I mean that sincerely. Those farmers have done a fine thing with their co-operative effort. I'm not one of those people who say co-operation is a bad thing. My company has notes from just about all the Yank farmers, and believe me, no one wants to see them succeed more than we do."

"But what if the money isn't recovered?"

"Well, sir, eventually—I say *eventually,* because we would do everything within our power to help—I suppose, eventually, there would have to be legal action. Some of those men haven't made payments on time in the past. Some are badly in arrears. We were all hoping this payment would get everyone on the square. Now . . ." Strider sighed again. "The prospect of having to take out court papers, and ask you to evict people —well, that's a dreadful prospect and I certainly hope it never happens."

This was getting him nowhere, Bradley thought. He changed tacks. "You've been around Emerald Canyon for a long time."

"I have," Strider agreed with a slight smile.

"What do you know about the way H. R. Yeager operates his business?"

"I know he's a good businessman, and a friend."

"I'm not suggesting anything here to the contrary. But I wonder if you have any recollection of when and where he might have gotten those two safes he uses."

"The big one and the little one both, you mean? Well, sir, the small one came here in the earliest days. A man named Brinker, I believe. He's dead now. The larger vault, I believe, was purchased in St. Louis and shipped in here about three years back."

"I'm wondering about the possibility of extra keys floating around."

"I doubt that, Jim. I sincerely doubt it. H.R. is very careful, and a good businessman. Anyone would attest to that."

"So you don't think there's much chance of extra keys?"

"No. I see little if any chance of such a thing. H.R. is much too careful."

Bradley saw that he was getting nowhere. A sense of defeat gnawed at him but he tried to ignore it. "Well, I'll keep checking leads. If you think of anything that might be helpful, let me know."

Strider nodded. "I hadn't seen poor Schmitz or McCollum for several weeks prior to today. I had hoped the meeting would be happy."

"Maybe it still can be," Bradley said.

"Do you think you have much chance of finding the money, Jim?"

"I intend to find it, all right."

"But the burglar must be long gone by now."

"We haven't had any strangers in town that I've seen. If that's true, then the money is still around here somewhere. I intend to track it down."

"But someone could have slipped into town without your knowing. I mean, that's possible, isn't it?"

"Maybe," Bradley admitted. "But I intend to start asking a lot of questions as of right now. If there was a stranger here, I'll find out about it."

"I wish you all the luck."

Bradley twisted his lips and resisted the temptation to say the obvious.

"I can have my sons ride around, tell the men to meet tonight," Schmitz said, finally breaking the long silence as he and John McCollum rode north from town.

"I'll let people in my area know," McCollum agreed glumly.

"We meet at my farm. At eight. *Ja?*"

"Phil, how could this have *happened?*"

"There was another key."

"Yeager said—"

"He lied."

"Why would Yeager lie?"

"*Ach,* I do not know. I only know it must be so."

They rode in silence for a while again, thinking about it.

McCollum was still partially dazed. He had imagined they were now on the high road to success. The loss of all the money put him and all the others back where they had been during the deep heat of midsummer: without resources, without genuine hope.

He did not have any idea of what they could do. For himself, Mary's advanced pregnancy made matters even worse. He could not move right now. There simply was no way. The aftereffects of the bullet wound made it imperative that she remain not only physically inactive, but as even-keeled, emotionally, as possible. What was he going to say to her? How could he explain it?

He knew, without analysis, that he was going to put it off as long as possible. Maybe tomorrow he could tell her in a gentle way, although that seemed impossible now. But at least he could pretend everything was all right for a few more hours. Maybe Jim Bradley would come up with something.

It seemed a very faint hope.

In the meantime, however, the other farmers had to be notified. They had to meet—try to decide what they could do. The prospect of crushing their hopes, seeing their faces when they learned the truth, was a painful one.

They had become very close, most of the Yank farmers. From separate individuals rendered suspicious and bitter by their individual fears, they had become surprisingly close-knit by their common goal and work together to haul water to their fields. As success came to their early hard work, their hopes had grown, and they had credited one another for it. So the work and the progress had made them have almost a . . . *family* feeling.

Remembering some of the days and nights of water hauling, the business meetings, arguments, discussions, jokes, the way they had all helped him when his shed was knocked down and Mary injured—it all came together to make John McCollum see how much they had gained together besides the financial base which had now seemingly been taken away. They had learned to sustain one another spiritually, and each man, knowing he had such friends, had been stronger for it, and a better friend to all the others. It had become a strengthful union that fed upon itself.

What was this disaster going to do to all that? To everything?

"What chance do you think Jim has of finding the money?" he asked.

Schmitz slowly shook his head. "I do not know."

"If we didn't take the money, though, then that means Yeager had to be lying, just as you said. We can make Jim see that. He can pursue it."

"How?" Schmitz asked.

"Make Yeager tell the truth!"

"It is not always possible to make a man tell the truth, John."

"But that's what we have to put our hopes on!"

"Yeager will say one of us took the money."

"That's ridiculous!"

"Or he will say we lost our key for a while."

"I know *I* didn't."

Schmitz turned in the saddle to look at him. *"Ja?"*

McCollum returned the older man's gaze, and in that moment he felt a sudden, swift doubt: He knew he had not been careless; *but could all this be Phil Schmitz's fault?*

After all, Schmitz was almost an old man. He had so many children, obligations, worries. He might have been careless during the trip to the markets outside the canyon, or during the time he was preparing for that trip—

At this point, the racing thoughts suddenly dead-ended with a new realization. McCollum saw how deeply his own faith in his friend had been sundered already by this unexpected adversity.

He thought: *I can't doubt Phil. If I'm willing to do that, we're finished: all of us.*

And at the same time, with a nightmare acuity, he saw the look in Schmitz's eyes. *Schmitz was simultaneously wondering about him.*

Was it a sign of how fragile the interdependence and faith of all the farmers might really be?

McCollum cast the doubt from his mind. "Neither of us could be at fault. It has to be Yeager or someone else. I'm sure of it."

"Ja?" Schmitz repeated.

"Yes. Now let's get going a little faster. We have a lot of people to notify." It did not seem enough to say. He added, "We got through everything else, Phil. We can work our way out of this."

In town Jim Bradley had been gone from the land office almost thirty minutes when the discrepancy finally registered. Smacking himself on the forehead with his palm, he hurried back to look Strider up again.

"Just one thing," he told the man. "You said you hadn't seen Schmitz or McCollum for some time. Was that right? Did I understand what you said?"

"That's correct," Strider said, his eyes narrowing. "Why?"

"How long ago was it that you saw either of them?"

"Let me think, Jim . . . a month at least. Together, that is. I might have seen one or the other since then, but not on a formal basis, I mean business, you know."

"How about earlier this week?"

"This week?" Strider appeared perplexed.

"The night of the fire, perhaps?"

"No. I certainly didn't see them that night. I was home, reading."

Bradley left the land office again, now deeply worried and puzzled. Schmitz had said they were meeting with Strider the night of the excitement. Now Strider denied it. Again, someone was lying. Yet no one had any obvious motive . . . unless Schmitz or McCollum was hiding something.

The obvious end of the line for the train of thought was one that Bradley would not quite face. He wondered if he would have to face it sooner than he wished. He felt a sour ball of dread building in his stomach.

In the hot, damp shade of the gully, Paul Lars stirred, sending up a cloud of flies that had been feasting on the blood from the terrible wound in his side. The first movement was almost involuntary, a twitch of awareness returning, but it was enough to send lacerating pain through his torso. Instantly he was fully conscious and hectically aware of just what had happened.

He lay very still, listening to the pain and the buzz of the flies, thinking of what a fool he had been.

He should have expected it, he thought, but even now it seemed unreal. He had not asked for very much, just a few more dollars. He had had it coming. He hadn't been ugly about it or anything. Samuel Kane could afford it for good work. My God, he could pay every hand on the place an amount a hundred times larger and probably not even miss it!

But Kane had obviously decided otherwise. He had given the order to Bing. The gunman would not have done this on his own.

So they had ridden here, Bing had gotten him totally by surprise, and had shot him at point-blank range.

There was no doubt the wound was very bad. Lars could feel the hole the slug had torn through his ribs. Somehow or other, the bullet had been deflected, however, probably going downward. He hurt badly deep down. He was not spitting blood. The lungs had miraculously been missed, along with the heart, and that was why he had regained consciousness.

Bing, he figured, had left him for dead and planned to come back later to get rid of his body. Already, judging by the sun through the trees, a number of hours had passed. Bing might be back fairly soon. Therefore it was time for Lars to get moving.

With a supreme effort, he held out against the pain while he climbed to his feet and leaned dazedly against the bank of the gully. Blood pulsed from his side. He got his shirttail wadded up and shoved into the hole. He was burning up and freezing at the same time, and things kept pulsing and getting black and then light, black and then light. He was fiercely dizzy and sick at his stomach, too.

But he could not stay here. He also could not go back to

the bunkhouse. He was in no shape to try to make a long ride, even if he could find a horse.

Town was his only hope. Town, and Jim Bradley.

Maybe he was going to die anyway, Lars thought, but it might almost be worth it if he could just get to town and tell Jim Bradley what he knew before death caught up with him. Kane had double-crossed him and Bing had been the gun. But by God, if he could just get to town somehow, just find Jim Bradley, they would both pay for what they had done. Somebody named Paul Lars might be a goner, but Kane and Bing would get theirs, too . . . if he could just hold out.

Lars started climbing out of the gully, and the pain was a real thing that cloaked him in yellow-red vibrations, making him gasp. But the anger was strong, too, and the pain made him angrier, and he got out of the gully and back onto his feet.

It was such a long trek into town.

Impossible.

But it *couldn't* be impossible. He had to get there . . . get Bradley . . . give him the story to get even with Kane and Bing.

Nothing else mattered, even if he finished killing himself in the process.

Lars started walking, shuffling along, trying to figure out a way to tune out some of the agony each step cost.

SIX

By late afternoon, when Freddie Smith came to the jail office for the start of his brief clean-up shift, Jim Bradley was beginning to see just how impossible the task of recovering the money really might be.

Freddie Smith, a lank black man whose lined face showed both the struggle of his life and the dignity born of the struggle, seemed to recognize Bradley's preoccupation; he began his routine sweeping and cleaning chores without conversation. Bradley remained at his rolltop desk for a while, moving around the pieces of paper that he had tried to write facts on for study. But they didn't make sense.

"Everything points in the wrong damned direction," he said finally.

"What was that?" Smith said, pausing in his sweeping.

Bradley looked at the black deputy. "This money theft."

"You got any leads, you think?"

"I've got some ideas, but that's what's bothering me. They all point in the wrong direction."

"Meanin'?"

"There's no way Phil Schmitz or John McCollum could be crooked!"

"Then," Smith said slowly, "it's got to be something else."

"I've talked to half the people in this town. There haven't been any strangers around. That means the money was taken by someone we know. But Yeager swears it wasn't him, and Schmitz and McCollum say the same thing, and I believe all of them."

Smith stared at him with thoughtful eyes. "What does that leave?"

"It leaves me in a hole."

"Naturally, there's ways to open some safes without no key. But that safe the money was in ain't like this one in our office, for example, all wore out."

"The door didn't open by itself," Bradley agreed.

"Comin' over here, I heard some folks talking. The news is all over town already. Everybody is talking about it."

"What are they saying?" Bradley paid attention because public opinion was always important in a town such as this.

"They're scared, a lot of 'em," Smith said.

"Scared?"

"Bound to be bad for business, some say. Bound to make people afraid to put their money away in the savings and loan. Bound to start some of them old foreclosures, people moving out, money drying up, stores in trouble, the whole thing."

"Well, it makes sense. I'm worried, too."

"Folks are real shocked. Bad crime like this, they ain't never had any of it. Now this happens, it shakes 'em."

Bradley nodded. "It probably makes them wonder where their town marshal was, too."

Smith said nothing.

"Right?" Bradley said.

The black man was evasive. "I wouldn't be the one to hear stuff like that."

It was true, but it was also evasive, just as Bradley had anticipated. There was still world enough of prejudice in Emerald Canyon; many people would not talk to Freddie Smith or any other black man as an equal, would not confide in him or even reveal innermost thoughts. But Smith was clever in his own quiet way, and always knew the pulse of the area. His evasiveness now proved that he had already heard rumbles of some kind . . . comments about where the marshal had been, or should have been, to stop something like this, the inevitable worried general questions about whether the job of law enforcement was getting done if a thing like this could happen.

Although most people in Emerald Canyon were perfectly honest, the links that held law and order together were always a little fragile here as elsewhere. The laws had to be good and just, and the enforcement had to be impartial, respected, and perhaps just a little feared. Jim Bradley knew that many people feared him, just a little bit. It was an image that a good lawman had to cultivate to some degree. He had to be aloof. It was why Bradley had few real friends, and probably never would have many.

Competence and aloofness, however, were only as strong as the record they stood upon. Give even the best lawman some bad luck—a rash of petty crime—and confidence could go fast. The wildfire spread of word about this devastating blow to the "Yank" farmers was enough to make Bradley's tenure a little uneasy.

Well, this was not something he could worry too much about. He had always had the feeling that the man who spent time building his personal defenses was not left enough time to do a good job. On the other hand, if you did a good job, the personal security took care of itself.

His concern was with the crime itself, and what he could do about it. Mentally he ticked off some facts:

—A commotion in town and an attack on him;
—A break-in at the savings and loan;
—Schmitz and McCollum saying they were with Strider;
—Strider denying it;
—Schmitz saying he had not been to the savings and loan for a long time;
—Yeager denying this;
—The missing money;
—The question of the keys.

They added up to a sum that he didn't like even a little bit.

He asked Smith, "Have you heard anything about anyone coming into any money?"

"No," Smith said.

"Well, we'll both be working tonight. There are a lot more people I want to talk with, and you never know. There might be something else in the wind."

"You mean another stealin'?"

"These things don't go in singles very often."

The door of the office opened and two men walked in. Both wore the beaten-up, dusty overalls of the farmer, together with heavy shoes and straw hats. Bradley recognized them and hid the fact that he wasn't pleased.

"Gentlemen! Come in! What can we do for you?"

The two men came over to the desk. The heavier man was of middle age, with a moonlike face and pork-chop whiskers. His companion was in his early twenties, pale, pinch-faced, slender, with cold eyes. The older, bigger man started the talking.

"We've been hearing about this thing at the savings, Jim."

"It's bad news, Mr. Dremmerton," Bradley said. "We're working on it—"

"From what we hear, the thief got away clean."

"We don't know that yet."

The thinner man spoke in a nasal twang. "You got a suspect?"

"Not yet, Mr. Wills," Bradley replied courteously. "But—"

"You know how bad this is for us Yanks?" Dremmerton demanded.

"I think I do."

"I guess it's what we get, trusting that damned German, that damned McCollum character. *They* messed this up."

"Their money was lost, too," Bradley pointed out.

"I'll tell you," Dremmerton said with a scowl, "we've got a meetin' tonight and I aim to speak my piece. It was stupid, wantin' that cash in a separate safe. They was careless, lettin' it get stole this way. Now we're all in the soup and we've got nobody to blame but ourselves for puttin' them in charge."

"I don't see how you can blame Schmitz or McCollum."

"You wouldn't," Wills snapped.

"What does that mean?"

"You're thick as hops with 'em. Always have been. But we just want you to know that *all* of us don't see eye to eye on any of this anyhow. We aim to speak our piece tonight. Schmitz and McCollum got us into this. I say it's time we had new officers in this co-op. I say they were criminally negligent, and somebody has got to pay, and they're it."

"How do you think they're going to pay?" Bradley demanded.

"I don't know, but they got to."

"Maybe you'd better suggest how, then."

"Look, there's no need to get on your high horse. We just came by to get the straight facts, and tell you them two don't represent the whole co-op. Every member has got rights—"

"I'm remembering that," Bradley said, hanging on to the thin thread of his temper.

"Well, see that you do."

"What do you mean by *that*?"

"I mean check *all* your leads. Phil Schmitz and John McCollum ain't angels. The way we hear it, their keys are the only ones that could have opened that safe. If that's so, then what do you aim to do about it?"

Bradley's chair thumped over as he got to his feet. "Are you saying they took the money?"

Wills's eyes widened and he backed off a step. "No need to fly off the handle, now."

"Is that what you're saying?" Bradley asked.

"I'm saying we want this thing checked out."

"All right, now let me tell *you* two something. I'm checking it out. I intend to get to the bottom of it. You two have been troublemakers inside the co-op ever since it was formed, from what I hear. Now your leaders are in trouble and you're the first to start circling, like a couple of vultures."

"See here," Dremmerton blustered.

"No," Bradley said, *"you* see *here.* If you have some evidence, you come forward with it. Until you do, you just keep your mouth shut. This means enough trouble without people like you trying to stir it up more for your own benefit."

"How could *we* benefit?"

"You'd like to head the co-op. Don't deny it."

"I could do better than they've done!"

"Maybe you could and maybe you couldn't. But don't come in here and politic to me, and don't try to intimidate me because I don't take kindly to it, mister."

Dremmerton grabbed Wills's arm. "Come on. We're wasting our time."

"Come back if you have evidence," Bradley called after them.

The door slammed.

Bradley took off his hat and hurled it against the wall. "Damn!"

Freddie Smith, who had been like a statue throughout the exchange, went over and silently retrieved the hat. Thoughtfully he dusted it off with his forearm and went over to hang it on a wall nail. "Looks like they're after them other two, all right."

"Let the slightest thing happen and the vultures start," Bradley said.

It was another of the things he had been harboring on the edge of consciousness, unwilling to face. Given a setback of this magnitude, the co-operative was too new, too fragile, to be sure of standing firm. People like Dremmerton and Wills would be busy now. Every real or potential enemy that Schmitz and McCollum had was sure to swarm.

It occurred to Bradley that the enemies, if they knew what he knew, would have already convicted his two friends.

"There's no reason why we can't meet occasionally to discuss the state of business and our community," Henry Strider said. "We have every right, and I mean that sincerely."

Strider, Yeager, and Thomas S. Simmons were together in the cramped back office at Simmons Feed and Produce Company. Strider appeared cool despite the muggy afternoon heat and his heavy suit coat, while Yeager, who had just complained that meeting might be dangerous, looked frizzled and soaked with sweat in his shirt sleeves. Simmons, immaculate and poised as always, sat behind his desk with fingertips touching under his chin.

"I thought we ought to make sure we're together," Simmons said.

"We know where we are," Yeager fumed.

"Yes, but I plan to go out shortly to report to our mutual business associate. Now as I understand it, Schmitz denied being in the savings and loan recently?"

"Of course he did," Yeager snapped, "since he wasn't."

"But you insisted otherwise to the marshal."

"Yes."

"Excellent. I assume Bradley also knows by now that the two men were not at your office the other night, Henry?"

Strider nodded. "It bowled him over."

Simmons allowed himself a thin smile. "But he hasn't taken any action."

"None that we can see."

"Fine. We'll give him his final clue at the proper time, then."

"Today?" Yeager asked.

"Perhaps. I must report first. Then the farmers will meet tonight, I understand. I assume you have made the proper magnanimous statement, Henry?"

Strider gestured affirmatively. "The land company is announcing that we'll give them all the time we possibly can."

"Excellent. I suggest that neither of you take any other action, and stay with the plan in every detail. If I have further news for you, I'll contact you at your homes late tonight. Agreed?"

Yeager nodded agreement, as did Strider.

Simmons got up from behind his desk. "I think I'll take a stroll for the air. It's very muggy. Do you think those clouds will make rain?"

As darkness began to gather, the rain started gently. Riding alone back toward the place where he had left Paul Lars, Bing hunched his shoulders to keep the drops from trickling down his neck. He was almost there and a man could not very well dig a grave in a long slicker, so he left it rolled tightly behind him on the pack.

Given the circumstances, Bing was pleased with himself. His day with the men had gone well enough and he had showed no sign of overconcern about Lars's absence. The men had shrugged it off, too. Now they were back around the bunkhouse and would not question Bing's fairly short absence. The rain was even helpful because it would obliterate tracks in very short order.

Bing watched carefully for signs of anyone else in the area as he approached the gully. His trained eye would have spotted any sign, however small. There were none. He led the horse along the grove of trees as the rain began coming down harder. He descended into the gully and followed it along. He turned a corner and came to the place.

It was a bad shock.

Bing, however, stared at the empty creek bed only a minute or so. His first reaction—rage at himself for uncharacteristic carelessness—was one he could not now afford and he recognized it at once. Squatting, he examined the pebbles and the earth for sign.

It was quite clear what had happened. He would have sworn that his shot took Paul Lars out permanently. He had seen the wound and knew what a .45 caliber slug did to a man at that range. Well, no matter. The bullet had bounced inside, somehow. Lars had not been dead after all. The man had, as wild as it seemed, gotten up and crawled out of here.

His pulse thumping, Bing considered courses of action. He had to find Lars and finish the job. That was obvious. Lars, however, had a gun and would not be tricked or caught off guard again. Bing did not like the situation even a little bit.

Closely examining the earth where trees had protected it so far from rain that would obliterate clues, Bing found the place where Lars had climbed out. Kneeling, examining the grass and brush with careful fingertips, he determined that his prey had gotten to his feet and started off on foot, staggering. He found, after a few minutes, a tree stump where the rain had not yet washed off the last signs of a bloody hand-print; here Lars had rested.

Bing considered alternatives again in light of this new information.

A man could live a long time sometimes with a terrible wound. Bing had seen men struggle for days when their insides were torn to pieces and there was absolutely no hope for recovery. On the other hand, he had seen soldiers who died from a minor injury, going into a strange shocked condition and sliding downhill with terrifying certainty and ease.

Lars obviously was not one of the latter.

The man was headed somewhere, even if he was as good as dead.

Fighting the rain and fast-encroaching darkness, Bing followed the signs as far as he was able. They led off at an angle to the northeast, not on a line that led anywhere near the Kane property. Was Lars wandering in a daze? It seemed unlikely; a man did not summon the will to walk despite such pain unless he had a very definite goal in mind.

Paul Lars's goal, then, had to be town.

Which could only mean he was trying to get to see the law, Jim Bradley.

Realizing this, Bing stifled an oath. He did not know how long ago Lars might have started his painful trek. On foot, ignoring terrain, a man could hike to town in four or five hours. If Lars could keep going, he might have made it in seven or eight hours even in his weakened condition. If he had started soon after the shooting, he might be almost there by now.

Bing made a decision between continuing to track and going on ahead. He had to assume he was right in guessing Paul Lars's motives. He had to get to town as fast as possible and await Lars's arrival . . . if it was not already too late.

There was no time to tell Sam Kane, even if Bing had had any inclination to do so. There was no time for anything but getting to town, heading Lars off, finishing the bungled job no matter how high the risk. Because if Lars talked, as much as he knew, more than Bing's safety was at stake and Bing knew it. The situation was desperate.

Bing brutally spurred his horse.

Jim Bradley was in his office alone, scrawling furious notes and questions, when Jean Reff appeared with the covered tray. He realized with a start that it had gotten quite dark outside while he was engrossed.

"You shouldn't have done that!" he protested as she placed the tray on the desk in front of him.

She uncovered a platter of steaming beef and beans, coffee, bread, and a big slab of pie. "If you aren't smart enough to eat, someone has to look after you."

Bradley noticed the raindrops clinging to her face and clothing. "Speaking of smart, haven't you ever heard about being smart enough to come in out of the rain?"

She chuckled and removed the shawl. "Be quiet and eat before it gets cold."

"I feel bad about this," he complained, stabbing with the fork. "You don't have time to look after me this way."

"Be quiet and eat, I said."

"What about your other customers?"

"Unless you've lost your watch along with your sanity, you'll see that it's past nine o'clock. There *aren't* any more customers. Everyone else has better sense than you do."

Bradley gave up. "Thanks. Really."

"Eat."

He obeyed. The food as always was delicious and piping hot.

"You've been a whirling dervish today," Jean Reff observed.

"That's a good description."

"I saw you churn up and down the street a dozen times."

"It felt like a dozen dozen."

"The money?"

"Sure."

"Have you made any progress?"

Bradley told her about it. "I finally got old Mr. Hoffsbradt to come into town and take a look at the safe," he concluded. "He used to be a locksmith, you know."

"Did you think he would see clues that it was broken into?"

"I don't know what I thought," Bradley admitted disgustedly. "What I really hoped, I suppose, was that he would say the lock was easy to pick."

"And?"

"To the contrary. It's a fine little safe and a good lock. The company is still making them. Hoffsbradt says there's no way to pick that kind of lock unless you're a factory man with special tools and dies."

Jean Reff's handsome face was solemnly thoughtful. "Is it possible, I wonder, that the factory keeps records of the key patterns? Could someone have written to get a new key from a serial number or something, and used that to open the safe?"

Bradley had to smile. "I thought I was brilliant when I thought of the same possibility about an hour ago. You came up with it faster."

"Can you find out?"

"I sent a telegram to the factory. I suppose I might get an answer in a day or two."

"You're very busy on other things, too," she said, looking at the notes all over the desk.

"None of it is doing me much good."

"You'll find who did it."

"I'd better. There's nothing more pathetic than an unemployed lawman."

"As if you would be out of work for long."

"I'm getting old. Jobs aren't easy to find."

"Poor grandfatherly thing."

They looked at each other and she smiled mockingly, fondly. There were many moments like this, Bradley thought. She encouraged him. Her liking for him was very clear, and her support was increasingly vital to him. He wondered if she had any idea how close he was, often—as now—to reaching out for her.

But he could not reach out. He had asked a woman to share the precarious life of a lawman, once. It had been a tragedy. He could never ask any woman to make that kind of sacrifice again. Jean was younger, was a beautiful and talented woman. She had made her own life since the death of her husband. She deserved better.

To avoid giving away the intensity of his need, he concentrated frowningly on the food. "This is good."

"Of course it is."

"I wish—"

There was a noise at the door.

The door flew open onto the night and the rain.

In the doorway was a startling apparition: a tall, stubble-bearded man, his clothing soaked with rain and mud and what might be blood. His face under the dirt was the color of chalk and his eyes blazed with crazed single-mindedness.

"Bradley—!" he gasped.

Bradley sprang to catch him or he might have sprawled.

He half-dragged the man to a chair against the wall and propped him in it. Turning to Jean he snapped, "Find the doc."

Without a word she fled from the office, leaving the door swinging open.

Bradley knelt beside the man. It was clear he was far gone. How he had gotten this far from wherever he had come from was astounding. The mud and rain soaked him, made him a slippery mummy. He had a pink froth on his lips and chin and his breath had a terrible rattle.

"Lars," the man choked. "I'm Paul Lars."

"Save your breath," Bradley urged. "Let me get you a shot of whiskey."

"No!" A hand clawed out and caught his arm in a savage grip, and Lars's eyes burned with intensity. "No time for that. Listen. I work for Kane—" A bout of coughing doubled him over.

Bradley rushed to the desk, found the whiskey bottle, came back with it, and poured some in the man's mouth. The wound in the side of his chest was incredible and he was still losing blood. He could not live.

Lars gasped as the whiskey burned down his throat, but splotches of color appeared in his cheeks.

"Night of the fire," he rasped. "Night the break-in—you got shot at—?"

"Yes. What about it?"

"It was me—"

"*You* shot at me? What are you telling me?"

Lars's eyes rolled back in his head. He grasped for the bottle. Bradley tipped it to his blood-stained lips. Nothing else would help him now. There would be nothing for the doctor to do.

Lars pushed the bottle away and shuddered as he swallowed. "Had to do the job," he said, his voice bubbly. "Want you to know. They got me back—you get them."

"Who?" Bradley whispered urgently.

A gunshot exploded with fantastic loudness in the room. From the open doorway—but Bradley did not turn because for just an instant he was staring at Lars and seeing the slug hit.

It threw the heavy man entirely off the chair and against the wall where he flopped like a rag doll and then slid downward, his eyes already rolling back. In the instant Bradley knew there was no second chance from this one—this one had caught him full in the side of the skull and the horror of it was etched in his mind as he spun by reflex, his own gun clearing leather.

Except for a puff of smoke lingering in the doorway, it was empty.

Bradley ran outside. The rain beat coldly against him. He saw no one—not in the dark alley that led toward the back of the building and not in the front yard that bordered the City Building.

Boots slipping on the grass, he ran to the street.

It lay empty, glistening mud, dark.

The assailant had gotten away.

Bradley ran back into the office and, steeling himself for the hideous mess, briefly examined Paul Lars. As much as he had seen in his life, he was back outside in the rain, retching, when Jean Reff returned with the doctor.

SEVEN

The rain had pelted down steadily all during the night, but with dawn the leaden sky churned under the motive force of stiffening north winds, the air grew sharply cooler, and the rain abated. Putting on a jacket against the unseasonal morning cool, John McCollum left his house quietly to avoid awakening his wife and slogged through the mud toward his storage building, intent on getting some pieces of tin to repair the slight leak in the house roof before the weather could turn worse again.

If the heavy rainfall meant the first touch of nearing autumn, it would have been more welcome under other circumstances, McCollum thought glumly. Ordinarily a rain like this, with a break in the terrific heat, would have made him ebullient; today he could only imagine such an emotional state.

Walking the downhill slope to the shed, he noticed how the remaining vegetables in the garden had been miraculously perked up by the rain. The okra looked gleaming green and fresh, and seemed to have literally grown six inches during the night. The tomatoes stood taller on their stakes. The late corn had been beaten down in places, but looked greener. The peppers and squash, which he had assumed were done for despite cautious rations of water from hauled cans of river water, also seemed brighter.

He could not see any damage. Rivulets gleamed where runoff drained downhill toward the gully and there was a deep sinkhole, like a tiny lake, in the field beyond. But the wind and rain had settled the dust, making the air invigorating in its near chill. The storm meant no more hauling of river water for a week or more at worst, and the crops that would be saved and extended in their productive period by real rain, rather than hauled water which never was quite the same, somehow, would be an unexpected bonanza.

For all the good it will do, McCollum thought bitterly.

He was at a low ebb emotionally. The meeting at Phil Schmitz's farm the night before had been far worse than he could have predicted.

It had been bad enough telling the other farmers of the loss of the money. Their reactions—dismay, shock, a sudden renewal of the old dulled apathy in the eyes of some—had hurt, deeply. Then had come the endless round of questions about what hope there might be of getting the money back, how it had been taken, who was responsible, what it meant in terms of the upcoming land payment dates, whether they should continue any of their fine, bright plans for wells and other irrigation projects—question after question from man after man, so many of them trying vainly to find some ray of hope, some way out.

Even worse had been the attacks on him and Phil Schmitz. He saw now that he should have expected these from the few who always hung back and second-guessed everything because they were not themselves in charge. But he had been at low ebb and badly out of emotional condition to handle what had been a stunning series of verbal attacks on him and Schmitz personally, as if they had *wanted* to lose the money . . . as if it were their fault.

Now he wondered if it was really worth going on.

Whether anything was worthwhile or not, however, he was determined at least to get the tin and the snips and fix the silly leak in the dugout roof. Presumably when things got bad enough this was one of the ways you tried to survive: by going about the routine chores as if nothing were wrong or as if something were right.

Reaching the shed, he walked around it, routinely checking

for signs of wind or storm damage. Finding none, he pulled a five-foot sheet of roof tin out from behind some planks and fence posts piled against the back, getting thoroughly wet in the process. Tossing the sheet of slightly rusty tin onto the ground in front of the shed, he got the door open and stepped inside to hunt the snips, hammer, and other things he would need.

It was musty-dark in the shed. Water had run in here and there, making the dirt floor slick in spots. He found the snips hanging on a nail and the hammer nearby. Going through a row of tin cans on a shelf, he got the nails he wanted and shoved a handful into his pants pocket. He would heat some tar in his bucket and he had a chunk of roofing tar around here somewhere.

Looking around the floor, he noticed that the feed sacks were shoved around in a way he had not left them.

Puzzled, he remembered the other time recently that the shed seemed to have been disturbed. Had the feed sacks been in this shape then? He didn't think so.

It seemed unlikely, this disturbance in the shed. Nothing was very far out of kilter, just enough that things looked messy and disorganized. It looked like someone had moved the sacks out from the corner, then put them back very sloppily. And yet there was nothing missing, and this could not be the work of a rascal like a coon because the sacks hadn't been torn open.

Grabbing the nearest sack, McCollum pulled it aside, thinking the chunk of tar might be behind it. It would not hurt to look, since he intended to rearrange things anyway. The building was much too small to allow for sloppy storage.

Someone messing in his shed was such a minor matter right now that it was almost silly, he thought, but it might be well to mention it to Jim Bradley. You could never tell about things.

He grabbed another sack and pulled it away. He thought there was nothing behind it.

Behind it, back against the wall, was a canvas bag of some sort. He didn't remember this.

Puzzled, he stepped over the other things and grabbed the neck of the canvas bag. It was secured with a piece of light twine which broke. The top spilled open. He peered inside. His breath caught. He fell to his knees and shoved his hands inside and made sure that it was what he thought it was.

"My God," he whispered.

Thunderstruck, he sank back on his haunches, staring.

His first reaction was utter disbelief. Was he still asleep and dreaming this? It was the kind of thing that happened in dreams, where logic went insane and nothing made any sense. But no, he was *awake;* feeling like a fool, he actually punched his arm, hard, hurting himself. He was awake and this was *real.*

It made no sense. How had this happened? What did it mean?

It was good, in one way. Unbelievably good. But *now* what happened? Someone had come into his shed and done this, but to what end? And where—he paused and frantically made sure of his estimate—was the remainder? This was not all of it. What would he do now?

Into his mind flashed memory of the harsh voices and hate-filled faces of last night. No one would believe anything this fantastic. If one problem was suddenly and inexplicably solved at least in part, then now he faced a personal crisis of even greater severity.

He could not just *tell* someone this. It would have all the earmarks of an obvious, clumsy lie. But to do otherwise meant cheating, running an even greater risk, betraying his friends. He was stuck, *really* stuck, and he patted at his pockets shakily, wishing for his pipe. But he had left his pipe at the house.

On legs gone to water, he stood up and hastily shoved the canvas sack back into the corner, tossing the other bags in front of it again. Despite the cool, he was sweating heavily.

He felt a near panic to get out of the shed and back up to the house.

Grabbing the tin snips and hammer—to hell with the tar right now—he shoved the door of the shed back and stepped outside into the gray morning wind.

Instantly he saw the horseman coming across the muddy yard directly toward his house, and already within hailing distance. He recognized him.

Jim Bradley.

Of *all* the times he did not want to see anyone!

Swinging out of his saddle, Jim Bradley tied his horse to the hitching post near the front door of the house. A glance showed him that the rain had done little or no harm to the sod walls that protruded a few feet above ground on McCollum's dugout structure. But McCollum, hurrying up from the storage shed, looked as upset as Bradley had ever seen him, even during the time of the bad trouble earlier in the summer.

McCollum was hurrying as if he wanted to put as much ground as possible between himself and the shed. His boots slipped in the mud and his face was a terrible pallor. When he neared the house and Bradley, his grin was a ghastly parody. "Good morning, Jim!" he called in a false tone.

"Sorry to bother you so early," Bradley said guardedly.

"No trouble, no trouble! I was just"—McCollum looked at the tools in his hands as if he had forgotten them—"I was going to fix a leak in the roof. You never fix a leak until it's dripped on you all night, right?"

Again the forced smile.

Bradley decided to bide his time and not confront the man about his obvious shattered state. "I came by, John, hoping you could show me that place where you hid your key."

McCollum frowned, seeming to have trouble getting his thoughts organized. "Yes. Yes, of course. Well, Jim, if you don't mind waiting just a little while, I mean, Mary isn't up yet—"

"I can come back later."

"No. Look, why don't we just sit here on this plank and visit a minute, and I'm sure she'll be awake enough for us to go in and have coffee soon. As a matter of fact, let me go in and check on her. I got up and sneaked out, wanted to get started on this." McCollum turned and hurried down the steps and into the house with the same disjointed nervousness he had shown walking up from the shed.

Puzzled, Bradley waited.

Within a minute McCollum poked his head back outside. "Mary is awake and presentable, Jim. Come in."

Ordinarily Bradley might have demurred and returned later. But his curiosity about McCollum's emotional state was too strong. All his instincts said there was something to be learned here, if he could learn it. The thought crossed the back of his mind that it had better not be what some people were already whispering as suspicion.

Going into the dugout house, he required a moment to let his eyes adjust to the dimness despite a lantern that McCollum lit with shaking hand. As usual the single room was very clean and neat. Mary McCollum lay in bed under covers, the child making her profile very large. She smiled. "Good morning!"

"Hello, Mrs. McCollum. Sorry to bother you so early."

"I'm glad someone came by to remind John to fix me my morning coffee," she replied cheerfully. "He won't let me do much for myself, so I just run him half to death."

"Good for him," Bradley said.

Putting water atop a newly stoked stove, McCollum asked, "What can we do for you, Jim?"

"In addition to looking at your hiding place, you mean?"

"Oh," McCollum said, his face changing. "I guess I forgot. I've got a lot on my mind."

Mary McCollum asked, "What's new on that man's death last night?"

"You heard about that?"

"You know how news travels."

Bradley nodded. "Not much, I'm afraid. He worked for Sam Kane. No known relatives. Kane will pay for burial. Says he was a good man, but inclined to shirk the hard jobs sometimes."

"You talk to Kane?"

"Late last night. It seems the man was named Paul Lars, and he had just walked off the job at Kane's place. Kane said he thought there might have been something bothering Lars. He speculated about gambling debts."

"You think his shooting was over gambling debts?"

"I talked with some of Kane's men. Kane said Lars was a heavy gambler, it was almost a sickness with him and he probably owed someone a lot of money that he couldn't pay. He said Lars had been asking for an advance on his salary. Kane's foreman, Bing, backed all that up. But the men I talked to said Lars didn't even get in their blanket-stakes games very often."

McCollum sat at the table, frowning. "What do you make of it?"

Bradley paused a moment, thinking for reasons he could not verbalize that maybe it would be better not to be quite so candid now with this man as he had been in the past. "I don't know," he said, which was a half-lie.

"John says it probably could tie in with the other trouble," Mary McCollum said.

"The theft of the money, you mean?"

"Yes."

Bradley turned. "Why do you say that, John?"

"Just guessing," McCollum said nervously. "No reason."

"I see," Bradley said, although he didn't.

Were his suspicions getting the better of him? Was he starting to think like some of the others? He didn't know. But things did not feel right here. Mary McCollum was acting normally. John McCollum was not—and even the trouble over the money could not adequately explain this. Bradley decided to try to learn what was going on.

"I heard your meeting last night was a humdinger," he said.

"You could say that," McCollum said.

"Dremmerton and Wills raised the roof."

"Right. Your sources of information are pretty good."

"My business. Tell me. What was said?"

"About what you'd expect. Phil and I were at fault. We were careless, let everybody down. The co-operative was a crazy idea to begin with, and now everybody will lose everything."

"How much support did Dremmerton and Wills get?"

"Some. I don't know how much. A few sided with them. Everybody was so upset—"

"Were there any votes?"

"No," and although this had to be crucial to McCollum, Bradley had the eerie feeling that the man was not thinking about it at all.

"What will the co-op do?" Bradley asked, his befuddlement deepening.

"Wait."

"And hope we can recover the money?"

McCollum did not reply for a minute. He looked around as if wishing the walls would fall away so he could vanish. Then he took a spasmodic breath. "Jim, I've got to talk to you. Privately."

"I like that," Mary McCollum said half-jokingly.

McCollum was on his feet. "I'm sorry. It won't take long. I'll be back in just a minute. Come on, Jim. Please," he added with a note of intense desperation.

Bradley followed him to the door, and outside.

"So there it is," McCollum said huskily in the shed. "I don't know how it got there—I don't know why—I don't know anything. I'm half out of my mind. I know it must look like I took it, and now I'm in a panic. I didn't know what to do. I even thought about keeping it hidden from you."

Shock trickling through his veins like melting ice, Jim Bradley looked at the contents of the canvas sack. It contained money—coins and greenbacks in about equal number—and there was no question in his mind about what it was. It was the money taken from Yeager's savings and loan.

"Is it all here?" he asked.

"No. It looks like about half."

"You're sure?"

"It isn't all there. I just found it when you rode up, but I know how much was in the safe and this isn't that much. It looks like about half of it, like I said—"

"Have you searched to make sure there isn't another sack in here?"

"There isn't anyplace for another sack." McCollum's voice cracked with tension. "Do you see anyplace where more money could be hidden?"

"I wouldn't have expected this here, either," Bradley pointed out.

"There isn't any more and I don't know how this—"

"Calm down, calm down. I believe you. Nobody is accusing you of anything."

"But my God, how does it look? If you *don't* suspect me, what's wrong with you?"

"I *know* you, John. That's how I know you didn't steal this money. And if you had, why would you be showing it to me now?"

"Because I lost my nerve, want to get out of it."

"Nuts. That's crazy and you know it."

McCollum stared at him with haunted eyes.

Bradley thought about it, getting over the initial shock. "Of course it might be that someone *wanted* it to look like you did it."

"That's what it has to be. But why go to all this trouble, and then not take the money?"

"I don't know. Why did someone take a shot at me in town the other night? Why did Paul Lars come to me? Why was he killed? You explain *any* of it to me."

"You don't think I stole the money?"

"Come *on,* John."

"No. I mean—you really don't? Because, when I saw it here, and then saw you coming, I knew you'd figure I had stolen it after all—"

"I've been in law quite a while," Bradley said wearily. "I know an honest man when I meet one. Now you've proved your honesty all over again by turning this sack over to me."

"But where's the rest? People will say I hid the rest!"

"People aren't going to say anything, because I'm taking this back to town and putting it in the bank in a regular account under the co-op's name, and if anyone asks where it came from, I say the investigation is still going on and that's confidential information."

"Can you get away with that?"

"We'll damned sure find out, won't we?"

McCollum stared at the sack of money. "It means a lot of the debts can be paid," he said slowly. "But I'll never get clear of this cloud over me. Not unless you can find out what happened."

"The money was taken and put here to discredit you," Bradley said. "That's as obvious as the nose on your face. Well, it isn't working. Just keep your mouth shut and I'll go on from here."

"I don't want Mary to know about this. In her condition—"

"Don't worry. I won't say anything to anybody."

"But what are we going to do *next?*"

Bradley waited a long time before replying. He thought it over and made sure he was probably right. Finally he said, "We'll have coffee. Then I'll ask you to ride over to Phil Schmitz's place with me."

"Phil's?"

"Right."

"Why?"

"If the idea was to make it look like you stole half the money, who do you suppose someone would want to make it look like stole the *other* half?"

"But then the thief wouldn't get anything!"

"Except a bad time for you and Phil Schmitz—which is, maybe, what this is all really all about."

"But that doesn't make any sense!"

"Tell me what part of this has, so far."

"You can't be right," McCollum said.

"Humor me," Bradley suggested.

EIGHT

H. R. Yeager was alone in his office at the savings and loan company when Jim Bradley walked in shortly after noon. Seeing the two canvas bags, Yeager knew immediately that things were going perfectly according to plan. But he showed nothing.

"Back for more questions, Jim?" he asked, going to the counter.

Bradley swung the two bags onto the top. "I have a deposit for you."

"All of that?" Yeager pretended it was a joke. "You must have really struck it rich, or has the town board voted a tremendous increase in your salary?"

"This is the money that was taken from the co-op's safe."

"Is that a fact! You recovered it already?"

Bradley's face was stony. "The best thing will be to deposit it in a regular account for the co-op. John McCollum and Phil Schmitz will be in later in the day to sign whatever papers are necessary, but that little safe in my office isn't very stout. Can you put it away in the meantime?"

"Of course I can! Of course! You found all the money! That's really fine, Jim. Congratulations. Who had it? Do you have the culprit under arrest, I hope?"

"The investigation is still going on."

"Where did you find this money?" Yeager touched a sack. "Say, these are heavy!"

"I think we ought to sit down and count it, Mr. Yeager. Then you can put it in the big vault and give me a temporary receipt."

"Well, that will be mighty fine, just mighty fine! Come on back here and we'll get right to work."

They took the sacks to Yeager's desk in the inner office and began counting. Because much of the money was already counted and held together with strings that included notes on how much each package contained, the paper-money counting went swiftly. Then the gold coins stacked up in dully gleaming cylinders as they worked on these.

"That's eleven thousand even right now, counted and on the table," Yeager said.

"Not much to go," Bradley said.

He was being very difficult, Yeager thought. This was not surprising; Bradley had obviously been handed a series of serious shocks. Yeager now began to suspect how Bradley was planning to handle it, and had to admire his courage and stubbornness.

"I'm sure a lot of people are going to be real excited, Jim. Do the Yank farmers know about it yet?"

"I've informed McCollum and Schmitz. They're spreading the word."

"Well say, that's truly fine! When do you expect to make an arrest?"

Bradley's eyes glinted dangerously. "Isn't that my business?"

"Of course! Of course! But say, this news is bound to travel fast. Everyone is going to be mighty excited. People will be asking over and over. I'm sure you must know that."

"I'll make a proper announcement at the proper time," Bradley said.

"Of course, of course. Like you say, it's your business. But folks will really clatter about this one, I can tell you! This is a great job you've done. There's bound to be a lot of curiosity. Seems strange that you got the money back, but nobody arrested yet."

Bradley's lips set, but he said nothing.

"You say McCollum and Schmitz will be in later to sign the deposits?" Yeager persisted.

"That's right."

"Fine and dandy. You know, Jim, your recovering this loot so fast is a real feather in your cap. Sure going to be a lot of talk! Yes, sir!"

"I think that does it," Bradley said, piling up the last few coins. He wrote some numbers on a sheet of paper.

"Our figures match. I'll get the receipt filled out right away. Let's just take this back and get it into the vault first, shall we? By golly, the last thing I would want would be for somebody to make off with any of this a second time, right?"

Still Bradley refused to rise to the jovial bait. He was still as taciturn as earlier. Yeager could not blame him for this, either. Yeager was intensely excited and anxious for Bradley to be gone so he could slip away and report to Henry Strider.

Leaving the savings and loan, Bradley went first to Jean Reff's café, where coffee and lunch took the edge off his gnawing hunger but did nothing for the tension. The café was crowded and he didn't have time for much talk with Jean. Before he could get out of the place, the rumor mill was in full operation and a dozen people congratulated him on getting the farmers' money back. The general air of jubilant congratulation only deepened his angry mood.

The visit to Phil Schmitz's house had only verified his worst suspicions and enormously complicated things for him. Schmitz had been first surprised, then indignant, then stunned when they went to his barn and found the second sack, containing the remainder of the loot, within thirty minutes. In the loft it was not even very well hidden and would have been stumbled upon within a day or two at most even if no search had been mounted.

"I do not understand this!" Schmitz had said.

"Someone set it up to make it look like we stole the co-op's money," McCollum explained tautly. "Jim and I talked about it on the way over here. Nothing else makes any sense."

"So now are we under arrest?" Schmitz asked.

"Don't be silly," Bradley told him.

Easy enough to say, Bradley thought now, approaching his jail office. And he intended to make it stick. But he had the feeling that the water was getting deeper with every new development. He did not like the feel of it at all.

All the evidence did point toward McCollum and Schmitz. If they had indeed taken the money, then lost their nerve and decided to take this crazy way of backing out on the theft, it would explain just about everything that had taken place so far. But it would not explain everything. It was against Bradley's instinctive trust of the two men, too. There was more here than he had uncovered so far.

Reaching the office, he reached out his key to open the front door lock but saw that it had already been turned open. Assuming Freddie Smith had come in unaccountably early, he walked inside.

It wasn't Freddie Smith. Bradley felt a quiet surprise.

"What do you want?" he asked.

Bing, Samuel Kane's foreman, had been caught standing in the middle of the largely barren office area. He turned quickly as Bradley entered, but the foreman's face quickly went from an instant of tension to a relaxed and almost lazy smile. A smile of this kind did not fit Bing's face.

"I just came by to pick up Paul Lars's things," he said. "Mr. Kane asked me to."

"Are you in the habit of walking into locked offices?"

Bing looked blank. "Locked?"

"How did you get in, anyway? And why?"

"The door wasn't locked, Jim!"

Despite his certainty to the contrary, Bradley glanced at the door. The lock showed no evidence of having been tampered with. But he knew he had locked it because he always locked it. Freddie Smith had the other key. Or could he have forgotten, anxious to see McCollum, and worried . . . ?

Bing was making a great show of wide-eyed concern. "Hey, I'm sorry if I walked in where I wasn't supposed to, Jim! I came by to see you and tried the door, and honest, it turned in my hand. So I thought you were here and came on in. Then you weren't, so I decided to wait awhile and here you are."

Angry without knowing precisely why, Bradley went to his desk with studied unconcern. He sat down and hiked a boot up on a corner, giving everything a sharp glance as he did so. There were no signs of tampering or searching.

"No harm done," he said.

"I'm sure sorry! I know how it is to have your personal place messed up. Living in a bunkhouse, a man learns to respect every other man's lockbox and bunk. Makes me madder than a hornet when somebody messes with *my* stuff. But the door was open, so I just came on in. Figured this is part of a public building, you know, and I'd wait."

The guise of concerned humility did not fit on Bing very well. He was a man Bradley had seldom spoken with, partly by choice. Bradley had pegged him as a former gunman or gang member, perhaps a killer, perhaps an ex-convict—or all of these things. None of that would have mattered if Bradley had felt Bing was now trying to be a different sort. Every man made his share of mistakes; every man had a right to try to live them down and go through the remainder of his life better for them. But Bing was not different now.

Although Bradley had no concrete evidence, he had always suspected that Bing was more than Samuel Kane's foreman; he was also, at least potentially, Kane's strong right arm, an enforcer if need be. Bing had the wide-set, dulled eyes of the bully and killer. The way he wore his Colt showed clearly that it was there for more than ornament or varmint protection. Many feared Bing with the same basis that made Bradley dislike him: a vague but unerring instinct for a dangerous and unpredictable person with violence in his past.

For these reasons, Bing's appearance here now, uninvited, galled all the more. But there was nothing to do about it. Bradley told himself his nerves were frayed and he was over-reacting.

"You say you came for Paul Lars's effects?" he said with an effort at control and civility.

"Right," Bing said.

"Kane is going to stand for the burial, then?"

"Yes."

"Seems mighty big of him, after Lars seems to have run off."

"Well, Jim, Lars was a good hand. If he had a problem and was scared or mad at somebody, maybe that was why he left. Maybe he hoped to get it straightened out, and then come back. Some guys do things like that."

"I suppose they do."

"Sam Kane is a big man that way, also. He takes care of his people."

Bradley reached into the bottom drawer of the desk for the small paper bag containing the pitiful few things that had been taken from Lars's body. He put the bag on the table. "You mentioned the man's enemies. Any idea who any of them might have been?"

Bing came over, took the bag, hefted it. "He didn't have much on him, did he? No, Jim, I don't know who might have been after him, or vice versa."

"Anyone at the ranch out there?"

"Not that I know about."

"Looks like you, as foreman, would keep tabs on things like that."

"I try to make the boys work. I stay out of their private lives. A man's business away from the job is his own."

"You're a very considerate foreman."

Bing gave him an icy smile. "I try, Jim. I surely do."

Bradley didn't move as the Kane foreman turned and clinked out of the office, taking Lars's things with him.

Lars had said he knew about events the night of the fire and commotions around town. Things had happened too swiftly for his exact words to remain in Bradley's memory, but the implications were clear enough: Lars had been involved, and directly so. Then someone had killed him.

The idea that Lars had died over a gambling debt or some other personal grudge was one that Bradley had not seriously entertained for more than a minute or two. Lars, he was sure, had died because he had been about to blow the lid off the entire insane scheme that was still, somehow, unraveling here. If he could find Lars's killer, he could begin tracking the twine back to its source.

But finding the killer was no more in sight than other leads that now seemed as illusory as faint smoke on a windy day.

Within the next hour, more than a dozen citizens came by the office to offer congratulations about recovery of the money. Most were genuinely pleased and relieved. A depression or even more serious trouble locally had been averted, in all probability, and everyone could see it. Most of the callers left puzzled, however, when Bradley refused to say anything about how the money had been found or who might be arrested for the theft. People liked to know these things. Talk was going up and down the street as fast as a gunshot as speculation mounted.

McCollum and Schmitz had been upset about the implications of the discovery, too. They had been surprised and concerned when Bradley insisted they keep quiet about everything they knew.

"It's designed to discredit both of you," he explained patiently, not for the first time. "All right. We keep still. Maybe that way we can force someone's hand."

McCollum had protested, "It's dishonest to lie about it, Jim. Those men in the co-op trust us. They deserve to know the truth because it's their money we're talking about."

"Just play it my way," Bradley had insisted.

He was sure he was right, and it was the only gambit he

could think of. But the pressure was severe. It got worse about 2:30.

"Have you made an arrest yet, Jim?" It was Thomas S. Simmons, the latest office caller, and his mood was gruffly pleasurable.

"Not yet," Bradley said.

"What's the state of the investigation?"

"Moving right along."

"Exactly how did you recover the money, if you don't mind my asking?"

"That's confidential right now."

Simmons's face darkened. "I can keep a secret, Jim."

"I know that. Right now it just has to be this way. Sorry."

"Well now, see here. I'm a member of the town board. We pay your salary, you know. I think I have a right to be informed."

Bradley took a deep breath and reached for his pipe.

"Well?" Simmons said after a minute.

"Sorry," Bradley repeated.

"You mean you won't tell me?"

"That's right."

"You're being unreasonable."

"I don't think so. If I'm going to handle the case, I have to do it in my own way. When the board hired me, that was among the guarantees."

Simmons's face blotched with color. "That doesn't mean running your office in secrecy. I'm not riffraff. The taxpayers have a right to know what's going on."

Bradley counterattacked. "Why is it you're so interested in *this* case?"

"What?"

"Why are you so—"

"I heard you, but I don't understand. I'm interested in good law enforcement. You know that. I've supported you right along."

"But why this case?" Bradley asked, probing. "Why not that cattle theft a few weeks ago, or the break-in at the store earlier in the week?"

"Those weren't of this magnitude and you know it."

"I still have to handle the case my own way."

"A person would think," Simmons said, "you had something to hide."

"Really?"

"Or you were protecting someone."

"Is that what *you're* saying?"

"No need to shout!" Simmons looked alarmed.

"If you've got something to accuse me of, you just spit it out."

"I didn't mean that! I didn't mean that at all! Here now. Don't ball up your fists that way."

"Maybe," Bradley seethed, "you'd better leave, Mr. Simmons."

"You're being unreasonable!" Simmons said, but from the door as he hastily retreated.

Bradley followed his shadow to the door and slammed it behind him.

The door did not, however, stay closed for long. More visitors came by. The town clearly was on its head over recovery of the money, and the same question was on everyone's lips.

It was the one answer Jim Bradley knew he could not let them have. He was reasonably sure it was a frame-up. But he had no proof of this. He had to keep the means of finding the loot a secret. He knew how bad things might become if the truth got out. People were people: they leaped to the nearest conclusion and were willing to believe the worst about anyone, no matter how good the suspect's reputation might be.

It occurred now to Bradley that people might even be quicker, some of them, to believe ill of a man like John Mc-Collum or Phil Schmitz, because they held positions of respectability and some power. It was easy to believe the worst of men in high places. It was easy to want to tear down those above you.

And he had to protect them.

Even though the slightest nagging doubt continued to bother him.

John McCollum rode into Emerald Canyon. It had taken some doing to keep Phil Schmitz at home. The old German farmer was too upset to come here and face the scrutiny and inevitable questions of the curious.

McCollum himself, not liking any of it the least bit, was resolved to maintain the silence Jim Bradley had ordered.

He rode the old mare toward the savings and loan. On a corner, some men he knew casually were talking in a group. One of them pointed at him and another broke off and walked over to intercept him.

McCollum reined up. The man, whose name was Roberts, worked at the blacksmith's shop. He looked neither friendly nor unfriendly.

"John?" he said. "Is it true all the money was got back?"

"That's right," McCollum said.

"John, there's a story going around town. I don't know how it got started, but it sure has people talking and guessing. Would you mind setting us straight on it?"

McCollum's insides tightened. "What's the story?"

"Well, sir, they're saying that money was found on your place. Can that be right? Have you heard anything about it?"

McCollum was so shocked that for a moment he said nothing at all, and had no idea how his face might be betraying his emotions. Roberts was watching him closely, but not necessarily antagonistically. McCollum knew he had to react.

He said, "I can't imagine how that story got started."

"Nobody knows, exactly. It's just going up and down the street. People say it's crazy, but I heard somebody say crazier things have happened. I said, 'Why would the money be on his own place?' But you know how these things get going."

Having no idea of what to say, McCollum licked sand-paper lips and kept quiet. Had Bradley talked? That was impossible. Who, then? *Why?*

"Where *was* the money found, John?" Roberts asked. "You know?"

McCollum got some control over himself. "I've been instructed not to say anything. Marshal Bradley is investigating."

Roberts's eyes narrowed. "You can tell us for sure it wasn't found on your place though, can't you?"

"I can—I can't say anything at all." McCollum knew how lame and damning this sounded. He added quickly, "To protect the investigation, we're not saying anything."

"You won't even *deny* it? Put the rumor to rest?"

"I'm not confirming it and I'm not denying it." Was that the right thing to say? How had it sounded? He was still completely at a loss after the unexpected question, and so many counter-questions were shooting through his mind that he wasn't thinking straight. He also had a sudden, sharp feeling of guilt—of fear. *I'm thinking like a guilty man,* he realized, and this compounded his confusion.

Looking at him very strangely, Roberts stepped back to let him pass.

McCollum tried to get things back together. "It's funny how crazy stories start sometimes."

"Yes," Roberts said, his lips turning down.

"I'm sure the truth will out."

Roberts said nothing. The suspicion was now coldly clear in his eyes.

McCollum clucked to the mare and thumped his heels into her sides. He had to find Jim Bradley.

Somehow, hearing the news from John McCollum, Bradley could not really be surprised.

"I guess that would be the logical next step," he said.

"I don't understand."

"We had a couple of possibilities earlier on what all this meant. But it's all starting to fall into place now and my doubts have gone down the drain." Bradley paused to fire up his pipe and then said through the smoke, "It could have been a real burglary at the savings and loan. The thief could have panicked or something. But that's out of the question now."

"I don't know how the word got out about where we found the money."

"Precisely."

"What?"

"The word was *put* out," Bradley said.

"Who did it? Why?"

"The 'why' isn't tough. You and Phil are leaders of the co-op. If you're discredited, the co-op might fall apart . . . or your friends like Wills and Dremmerton might take over the leadership."

"They'd ruin it!" McCollum said.

"Precisely, as I just got through saying."

"This is all aimed at destroying our organization, then."

"It has to be that."

"Who?"

"Consider who could have started the story about where the money was found."

McCollum looked blank.

"I mean," Bradley explained, "consider how many people knew. You. Phil Schmitz. Me. *And* the thief."

"How does *that* help?"

"It helps because the thief had to know it was possible, at least, for the money to have been found at your place. That means he has to have known I was out your way, and he has to have known when I returned the money to town, in order to know when to start the rumor that I found the loot where I did."

"I'm not following you at all," McCollum admitted.

"I came back to town," Bradley said. "I handed the money

over to H. R. Yeager. Within thirty minutes the story was
going up and down the street about how I recovered it 'somewhere.' Now the story is going around about how I found it.
Yeager let the first rumor out. I think he also started the
second one."

"Why?"

"That's the hard part. But he's old guard around here. He
has dealings with Sam Kane. Kane and the people he associates with stand to lose the most by success of you farmers.
Hell, we've known that all along."

"You think they're setting this entire thing up to ruin us?"

"Yes. I also think that burglary at Yeager's was as phony
as a three-dollar bill. That window had never been opened far
enough to let a man inside. I thought I was sure of that, but I
went by a while ago and checked it again from outside. I've
been trying to put the rest of the pieces together, and when
you came in here saying the story about how we found the
loot is circulating up and down the street, it fell into place
for me.

"Yeager took the money out of the safe. He probably had
a duplicate key all along. If he had one made recently, I've
got a telegram coming home to roost in the next day or so
that will prove it. Either way, he got the money, got it out of
there, got somebody to put it in your place, and Phil's."

McCollum rubbed his eyes as if in disbelief. "But you can't
prove any of it!"

"Probably not," Bradley admitted. "And he had help, certainly, and I can't pin those people down, either. But this new
rumor tears it as far as I'm concerned. I can't sit around any
longer and wait to see what they do next."

"What are you going to do?"

"You'll see. You just get on over there to Yeager's and
get enough cash money out to pay Strider Land Company."

"Now?"

"I don't mean tomorrow."

"But I don't know if I'm authorized—"

"Do it!"

"If you say so, I will, but—"

"Sorry I barked," Bradley said. "But I want you to move. Because as soon as you've done that, I'm making a move of my own."

McCollum frowned worriedly and leaned across the corner of the desk. "Jim, I don't want you sticking your neck out any more for us. You've already taken too many risks."

"Nuts. Do what I tell you."

"You could really endanger your own reputation."

"I don't see how," Bradley lied.

"You don't know that Phil and I didn't actually steal the money!"

"Nonsense!"

"But you don't have any evidence!"

"Listen," Bradley said. "I see what I have to do now. You just let me do it."

McCollum stared at him.

"All right?" Bradley asked.

McCollum nodded.

"Go do it," Bradley said.

McCollum, his head down with worried thought, turned and left the office. Bradley sat staring at the vacant doorway for several minutes.

He knew that the plan which had suddenly begun to develop in his mind was tissue-fragile, as dangerous for him as for the others. But the whole scheme seemed clear to him now and it was unwinding with such clockwork ease and rapidity that he could only change the pattern by drastic action.

It was very clear that the plan in his mind could backfire. He was taking the all-out gamble that the unexpected on his part would force adjustments on the other side—somehow bring them out into the open. If his element of surprise were not complete, their counterattack could destroy him.

It was a frightening prospect. He had gotten used to this

office, to this desk, the little safe in the corner, the straight chairs, the way voices leaked through the wall and ceiling from the City Building sometimes. He knew the view from the open door and the way shadows moved across the side lawn in the afternoon. He knew the sights and sounds and odors of this little town, and the people. It was a good place.

More than anything else, however, he thought about Jean Reff.

Perhaps he would never get up the courage or arrogance or desperation to come across with what was on his mind to Jean. It was so unfair to ask her to risk heartbreak again. A lawman should not have a woman because even in the best times he had to leave her alone too often while he went about his work, and at any time a freak chance could make her a widow, broke and alone and grieving again.

In the past weeks, however, Bradley had begun to feel that one day he might get up the gumption to speak his mind to her. He thought he knew how she would respond. And he yearned for that response. It had been a long time since he had been with a woman. It had been even longer since he had been able to risk expressing love.

Now, however, he might be throwing this chance of possible happiness away, too. If his plan backfired, he knew he might lose his job and possibly even more. Disgrace and the possibility of death lurked behind the doorways of this scheme, and he did not want to risk it.

He brooded about it, but saw no alternatives—not if he was to stay in this chair and be The Man.

After a while he left the office and walked to the front lawn of the City Building. New rain clouds were scudding in and the breeze was almost cold. Several people went by, smiled at him, and mentioned recovery of the money. He saw the questions in their eyes.

There would be more questions soon, he thought.

He was able to observe it when John McCollum left Yeager's with the money for land payments. McCollum was not inside the Strider Land Company long. When he came out again, worried-looking, he went to the general store for a few minutes and then came out carrying a small bag of food. Bradley saw, although McCollum didn't, some of the covertly suspicious glances shot McCollum's way by passersby.

McCollum got on his old mare and rode out.

Bradley considered his plan for another minute or two, seeing just how desperate and risky it really was, but also seeing that the only alternative was to sit back like an old bull buffalo waiting for the next shot to strike into the heart.

He took a deep breath of resolution and walked down the street, his boots slipping in the drying mud. He went into Yeager's savings and loan.

This time Yeager was not alone. His assistant was also there. But it was Yeager who came to the counter, smiling.

"What is it this time, Jim?" he asked.

"You're under arrest," Bradley told him.

NINE

From the vantage point of her café, Jean Reff was able to see the whirlwind Jim Bradley reaped with the arrest of H. R. Yeager, one of Emerald Canyon's foremost businessmen.

At first it was excited talk that went down the street like wildfire: astonishment, incredulity, shock. Then all the crazy rumors started, being repeated in the café by excited storekeepers and merchants. They said Yeager had tried to steal the money. They said he had had it all along. Then they said his arrest was for something else entirely.

"Jim file charges yet?" someone asked.

"Nope. Nothing."

"When's he gonna?"

"I dunno. I heard—" Another crazy rumor that made no sense.

Swamped with customers, Jean could do no more than listen, and hurt.

She did not understand what it all meant. Jim had said nothing about this to her. She hoped desperately that he knew what he was doing. But a doubt tickled the back of her mind.

Like Jim, she liked and trusted both Phil Schmitz and John McCollum. But if the earlier rumors were true, the evidence appeared to indicate that they, not H. R. Yeager, might have had something to hide. She hated this doubt about trusted friends that crept into her mind, but it was there nevertheless. Had Jim made a terrible mistake here? Was he attacking an innocent man to protect a friend who was guilty?

The doubt assailed her. She kept looking at the clock as

the afternoon rushed along, hoping for some kind of a lull so she could go to the jail and talk to Jim for herself. But no time became available.

The evening rush had just begun when the latest report came in, a man named Banner who told the crowd excitedly, "Town board's havin' a special meetin'! I heard they called Jim Bradley an' the judge an' Luke Ball, the board's lawyer."

"Heckfire! Let's git over there!"

"Can't. Closed meetin'."

"What kind of thing is that? They can't hold a closed meetin'!"

"They sure can," Banner said firmly, his eyes glinting with excitement. "They can—when they're talkin' about hirin' or firin'."

Luke Ball, the youthful town board attorney, came into Jim Bradley's office with a scowl of worry etched into his features. He remained in the open doorway almost as if he were afraid to come farther. Nightfall made the opening behind him a gray blue.

"The board is getting set to start, Jim," he said.

Bradley blew out a lungful of air. It was all going very, very fast, and not exactly in the directions he had expected. It hadn't taken long for word of Yeager's arrest to get up and down the street, as he had intended. Then the angry visits and questions from Henry Strider, Thomas S. Simmons, and certain other leading citizens had also been predictable. He had really, however, expected some shocked interim after that point. The speed with which a town board meeting had been set up worried him.

"Are they ready for me?" he asked Luke Ball.

"That's what it's all about," Ball replied.

Bradley shoved away from the desk.

"Look, Jim," Ball said quickly. "The judge is up there, too, you know. All you have to do to clear the air is explain the charges to me, and I can quick-like draw up a formal complaint. We can walk up there together and file it with the judge. That will take a lot of wind out of their sails."

"I'm not ready for that yet," Bradley told him.

"Hell, Jim, you're *asking* them to dismiss or suspend you!"

Bradley felt a gusty chill in his belly. "Are they that far along already?"

"I don't know. But you're just asking for trouble. The way you're going about this thing is too high-handed. All people want is reasons—formal charges. You can't arrest a man like Yeager and just say you want to hold him for investigation. It's out of the question!"

"You're the board's lawyer," Bradley said, "not mine. Why this concern?"

Luke Ball's face worked. "I've . . . thought a lot of things over, Jim. You've been good for this town and the people. You've been square. I—I've come to like you, dammit. Now are you going to throw everything away? It's crazy!"

It seemed like a very sincerely intentioned speech, a true one. It startled Bradley a little. He saw suddenly that he had a friend here whom he hadn't even recognized up until now. He wished he could let Ball in on what he was really trying to accomplish. But he couldn't.

"I'll go see what they have to say," he told the young lawyer.

"Jim—!"

"Let's go."

They walked outside and around the building. The rain had held off, although clouds covered the moon and stars. In the cool wind a handful of people stood around the front steps to the City Building. Their muttered conversations stilled as Bradley and Ball walked through them and up the steps into the building.

It was quiet inside and the hallway was dark. At the far end, the lighted doorway of the boardroom was a bright yellow rectangle. This was the way things happened, Bradley thought; it might have been an ordinary visit to the board's chambers to talk about pay vouchers or jail food bills. Instead, this time everything was probably on the line.

"I still say you're making a mistake," Luke Ball muttered as they walked down the corridor.

"It won't be my first," Bradley said.

They entered the room.

Six men were already there, and all stood around the long table at the front of the room, flanked by a pair of American flags. Bradley recognized all of them at once: the board members, Strider, Simmons, and T. L. Bailey; old Judge Johnson, and two Main Street merchants, a clothier named Hopkins and the gunsmith, Pradaro.

Henry Strider glanced up at Bradley's and Ball's entrance. "I see we're all here. Good." He glanced at Hopkins and Pradaro. "If you two gentlemen will go watch the outside doors to assure privacy, as we suggested, the board will get going on this thing."

Hopkins and Pradaro brushed elbows with Bradley as they moved past him in the narrow aisleway between empty folding chairs. They silently closed the door at the back of the room as they departed.

Strider motioned for his fellow board members to take chairs at the table. "Sit at the end there if you like, Judge."

Judge Johnson, a leather-faced old man reduced by some lingering illness to skin and bones, shook his head stubbornly. "I'll stand."

Strider pointed to a couple of the chairs in the vacant first row. "Luke. Jim. Sit there if you like. Nothing formal about all of this." His smile was antiseptic.

His pulse stirring, Bradley sat at the right of the aisle and crossed his legs. He needed his pipe and started patting around for it. He had left it at the office. It was, he thought, a hell of a start. He noticed that Luke Ball cautiously put the space of the aisle between them. The board members fussed with note pads and pencils, and Judge Johnson stood his ground at the right end of the table, moving back and forth a little like a tall tree in a strong wind, glowering.

"All right," Strider said, folding his hands on the table and meeting Bradley's eyes. "No sense beating around the bush here, eh? We want to know where we all stand on this investigation of the disappearance of the Yank farmers' money."

"To put that another way," Simmons chimed in easily, "we're disturbed, Jim. We're disturbed about developments of the past few hours. We have to answer the voters of this town and we need facts."

T. L. Bailey, a thick man who habitually frowned from beneath a luxuriant shelf of eyebrows, turned his pencil over and over on the table. "This seemed like the best way to get the information we have to have."

"No one wants to hamper your work," Strider added. "We mean that sincerely. But frankly, Jim, your conduct has puzzled and upset all of us here."

Bradley hesitated before replying. He saw that Bailey was ill at ease, perhaps less sure of the situation than the other two board members. This was not surprising because Bailey was not close to the others, or at least not as close as the other two were. Bailey's actions might be pivotal since he apparently was starting the session uncommitted. It was important to make sure Bailey saw what the issues were.

"I know there's a lot of excitement," Bradley told them. "I've had to do what I've done to make progress on this case."

A vein stood out on Strider's forehead as his anger almost got away. "You've arrested one of this community's leading businessmen and thrown him into the jailhouse."

"I'm aware of that."

"What is he charged with?"

"You have the judge here. You must know that no formal charge has been requested either from him or through the town attorney, here."

Luke Ball shifted his weight uncomfortably. "What they're getting at, Jim—"

"We can speak for ourselves, counselor!" Strider snapped.

Bradley said, "I see what you want to know. I'm sorry. I'm holding Mr. Yeager for investigation—"

"You can't just arrest a man out of his business and hold him for no specific charge!"

Simmons leaned forward. "We're reasonable men, Jim. You see what deeply troubles us. Your actions have been high-handed and illegal."

"Not illegal," Bradley corrected him.

Simmons glanced questioningly at Judge Johnson.

The judge scowled and cleared his throat. "Marshal has a right to hold a prisoner in detention up to forty-eight hours for investigation. That's the law. He's inside his rights."

"What," Strider asked, "if the man is innocent of a crime?"

"Then the man has a right to sue for false arrest," the judge replied in his tissue-paper voice. "And collect, I reckon."

"What's your case against H.R.?" Strider asked, turning back to Bradley.

"I'm not ready to state it."

"This board pays your salary and I'm directing you to answer me."

Bradley felt their eyes upon him and he was aware of the pulse in his throat again. They had moved to the heart of it very swiftly. He wished there were some other way. But if he was going to smoke anyone out, it had to be this way or not at all.

He said, "I'll have to decline to answer. Respectfully. I have my reasons."

T. L. Bailey's bushy eyebrows knitted over the bridge of his nose. "Jim. Listen. The rumor is up and down the street that you found that money at McCollum's farm, or maybe Schmitz's. People are saying you have evidence that your own friends did it, took the money, and you caught 'em. Now you arrest H. R. Yeager. I don't know what to believe here. What are you going to tell us about it?"

"I know how the money was taken," Bradley said, extending his gamble. "I also know who the guilty parties are. It won't be long before there will be more arrests."

Simmons asked, "Where did you find the money? *Did* you find it at McCollum's place? Or Schmitz's?"

"Yes."

It shocked them.

"You admit that?" Strider gasped.

"Yes."

"If you found money at those men's farms, why have you arrested someone else? That doesn't make any sense!"

T. L. Bailey leaned forward, his face troubled. "This is a very serious matter."

"Of course it is," Bradley said.

Simmons said, "McCollum and Schmitz are your friends."

"Meaning?"

"People can say you're protecting your friends."

"I understand how it may look."

Bailey's frown deepened. "Do you have evidence to support your actions?"

"I'm not prepared at this time to release evidence. I'll do so when the time comes."

"Jim, you're making it extremely difficult for this board. On the one hand you have evidence—things we all know about —that point toward McCollum and Schmitz. I've been told some of the Yank farmers are already incensed about this situation, so not even the co-operative supports your friends a hundred per cent. Now you arrest H. R. Yeager and you refuse to talk about that, either."

Bradley refused to shake Bailey's worried gaze. Bradley knew that Bailey had to be feeling intense pressure. He was, after all, one of the business community. That in itself tied him somewhat to the other two men at the table. Bradley understood the man's worry, and wished there was something that could be done about it. But the issue had to be forced now. The plan, parts of which Bradley could not even try to guess at, had to be thrown out of kilter. So he said nothing.

Simmons traced a doodle on his note pad and then looked up. "The board asks for a discussion of your evidence against H.R."

"I'm sorry."

"The board asks for your evidence against arresting Schmitz and/or McCollum."

"I can't give you that at this time."

"You refuse?"

"Respectfully."

Simmons's face darkened. "Thank you, Marshal. I believe we can excuse you." He glanced at his fellow board members for agreement.

Bailey said slowly, "Jim. Do you know how bad this makes you look?"

"I've got to do my job the way I see fit," Bradley said.

"You're excused," Simmons snapped.

Luke Ball, silent for so long, got to his feet. "Gentlemen, I'm sure Jim has his reasons, and, given some time—"

"Thank you, Luke," Strider said shortly.

Bradley turned for the door. Judge Johnson made a move as if to follow him.

"Please stay here, Judge," Simmons said. "We may have the need for a legal opinion here."

Darkness had fallen outside the City Building, and Bradley made his way quickly through the small gathering of citizens whose conversations died as he went down the porch steps and into their midst. He sensed the curiosity and latent hostility in their glances. He had friends here. He also had acquaintances who would be as quick as anyone else to change their generally favorable opinion of him if evidence pointed to the contrary. The law functioned by public consent. No man could make a really bad law work. No lawman could stay in business long if public opinion swung harshly against him. Walking quickly down the street, Bradley knew he was risking everything at the center of his life.

He could not, however, see any other way. He had to move quickly now if he was to capitalize on his surprise, and the uncertainty that he knew a sudden arrest would also be working inside H. R. Yeager by now.

He went to the café, where only three other men still lingered over late coffee. Jean Reff, her eyes instantly worried, met him at the far end of the counter and spoke in a low tone.

"What happened at the meeting?" she asked.

"They had questions, that's all."

"Jim, you're lying." She was *very* worried.

The harshness of his predicament, however, made Bradley harden his expression even to her. He could not afford to show his feelings now. Maybe he would never be able to show them to her now.

"Jean, I need a jail meal for my prisoner. Whatever you have that you can put together fast, please."

His hands were flat on the top of the counter. Jean Reff was a woman of an essential dignity, a concern for her privacy as an individual. She was not the kind who ever showed emotion in public. Now, however, with an instinctive sympathy, her hand stole out and covered one of his. Her hand was warm, and pressed his fingers urgently.

"It's taken a new turn, hasn't it?"

"I'm in a hurry, Jean," he said stiffly.

She reacted almost as if he had slapped her face. Her hand recoiled sharply and her face changed color. "I see. I'm sorry." She turned away abruptly and went to the back counter and stove area.

Bradley knew the other men had covertly witnessed the exchange and were now watching him for reaction. His face heated slightly. The turmoil in his chest, however, was far greater.

It happened like this so often. In the times of worst stress, a man had to be on his own, had to cut off even those closest to him, because only a single man, alone, could have the freedom to do what had to be done.

It had always been that way with him. There would always be times like this when he had to stand by himself and make the lonely decision. Possibly even a John McCollum could not fully understand this sort of isolation.

He had done it now, however. Rumors had already turned some of the town. The farmers were split. The board was against him by a vote of at best 2–1. Now to maintain the integrity of his plan—and his sanity—he had had to cut off Jean, too. Now he was almost completely alone. It was not a new feeling, but it never felt any better than it did right now.

Stiff-faced, Jean brought back the metal plate and cup with steaming contents. She placed them on the counter top with a brusque sound. "Twenty cents."

Reducing him to a paying customer and nothing more.

He put the money on the counter, picked up the two containers, and left.

Freddie Smith was at his desk in the jail, idly going through Wanted circulars. Bradley put down the food long enough to hand the black man the key to the shotgun cabinet.

"Freddie, I'll ask you to go the rounds first tonight to shake doors."

Smith looked up warily. "Meeting over?"

"My part."

"Everything all right?"

"I suppose."

"We filed charges on Mr. Yeager yet?"

"Not yet, Freddie."

The deputy wanted to ask, but had the dignity to restrain himself. He left his desk and went to the gun cabinet, unlocked it, and was getting down a shotgun to take on his alley rounds when Bradley carried the food and coffee through the doorway into the adjacent cellblock.

A lantern flickered on a nail in the stone wall of the corridor. Its pale light gleamed blackly off steel bars and barred doors that stood at geometric angles, open into the hall. Only the one cell door was closed, the far-end cell. A furtive, frightened movement in the dimness betrayed H. R. Yeager's presence.

Bradley placed the tin plate of food on the floor and slid it under the bars. "Supper."

Yeager, collar open and face a ruin, came to the bars. The shock of arrest and the relatively brief time alone in the cell had worked a terrible change in him. The bluff confidence was eroded and a stark fear shone in his round eyes.

"Why have you done this to me?" he asked thickly. "You can't do this. I demand to know what charge is being filed."

"Your coffee." Bradley held the cup between the bars.

Yeager stared at it, then at him. *"Why are you doing this?"*

"Take the coffee."

Yeager made a choking sound, took the cup, carried it back to the steel bunk, shuffled back again for the plate of food, and then sat on the bunk huddled over it.

Bradley watched him, forcing himself to ignore any impulse toward sympathy.

Finally Yeager looked up. "You're going to be sorry about this." His voice cracked with anger. "This high-handed treatment will lose you this job, and by the time I'm done you'll never get another one."

Outside, the door closed quietly as Freddie Smith left on the rounds.

"You know why you're here," Bradley told Yeager.

"Have you filed a charge? You haven't filed anything! You don't have a case. Why are you doing this to me? I'm not a well man. The doctor says I have a heart condition."

"Maybe you should have thought about that before you got into this mess."

"I don't know what you're talking about!"

It was said strongly, with only the slightest tremor. Yeager had strength. He was off balance and frightened but he was fighting, too. It was up to Bradley to break him down.

"Mr. Yeager, you took that money from the co-op's safe."

For the smallest part of a second Yeager's upraised face was absolutely without defenses as the words registered on his brain. Watching him intensely in the dim light, Bradley felt a leap of intuitive certainty. *It was true.*

Instantly Yeager's face closed. "You're out of your mind!"

"No."

"Those two Yanks had the only keys. I've told you that. Why would I take money from my own establishment? What proof do you have?"

"I know exactly what happened and how it was done," Bradley lied. "And I know why. But you made some serious mistakes."

Yeager's eyes darted furtively. "I don't believe any of this." But his voice betrayed him.

"You took the money."

"No."

"I know you weren't alone. The plan was to ruin the co-operative and the people in charge of it, wasn't it? And then, if you could get me in the process—"

"That's crazy!"

"The only trouble," Bradley went on as if he knew everything and could be glacially calm about it, "was that you took the biggest chance. The others set you up."

"Set me up?" Yeager whispered.

"If anyone was to be caught, that man was you. You were the one they could afford to lose if things went wrong."

"No. No."

Bradley had to press his advantage. He went back to something he had learned many weeks ago, on a secret trip to the county seat. "You know how it works when someone is set up. Remember the Culbertson deal?"

Yeager's throat made a rattling sound.

"Culbertson owned the bank," Bradley told him. "He never

understood how that sudden demand for cash wiped him out. He would have had to go to the county seat and dig awfully deep in those file cabinets to learn how you and Simmons and three or four other men went together with Kane and created a situation where all the major depositors made seemingly accidental demands in the same two days. You even got the town board in on that one, according to the papers. The payroll cash demand for the street grading project was the last straw that put Culbertson under, and gave you a clear path to setting up your new savings and loan."

"I don't know how you learned about that," Yeager said, "because you weren't even here. That was long ago—"

"I've made it my business to investigate how you and your friends work."

"There was nothing illegal—"

"That's right. But you set it up so that Culbertson would be the only real loser if there had to be a loser. And that's what the others have done to you now. You took the big risk. You stood to be caught, if anyone did. And you have been caught. You were set up."

"No. I wasn't set up. I haven't done anything."

"Have it your own way," Bradley said. "Take all the punishment alone."

He turned and walked out of the cellblock.

"Wait!" Yeager called weakly.

Bradley ignored him and went to his desk in the office room. He sat down and purposely slammed some drawers to make sure Yeager knew he was abandoning him again.

There was a thick silence from the cellblock.

It looked like it was going to work, Bradley thought grimly. Yeager was thoroughly frightened now. Give him a little while to try to chew and swallow food that would taste like cotton. Let him ponder the fact that the old Culbertson transaction was known when he had imagined that was buried forever. Let him think about *what else* might be known . . . what else could be used against him.

He would crack, Bradley thought.

There was nothing to do now but wait a little while to let Yeager's terror build, feeding upon itself. Bradley turned to the papers that Freddie Smith had been examining, and tried to concentrate on them. At the bottom of the pile were some of the notes he had made earlier about the events leading up to, and following, the vanishing of the money. He looked at these.

There was still the matter of the telegram to the safe company. He allowed himself a brief hope. The chances were very great against any help from that source. But men in power sometimes performed with amazing arrogance. It was worth hoping, anyway. . . .

In a few minutes the door of the office opened. Old Judge Johnson, his face a thundercloud, came in.

"What happened?" Bradley asked quickly. He saw that it had to be worse than he had anticipated.

"Going to be a hearing," the judge said. "In the morning. Ten o'clock."

"What kind of a hearing?"

"Board's going to decide at that time whether to suspend you from office."

"*What?*"

"Suspend you from office. That's the words they used tonight. What it means is fire you. Same thing. They know that. Talked about it."

Bradley leaned back in the chair, surprise prickling through his body. "I didn't think they'd go that far. Not this fast!"

"They're hot. Real hot. Bailey said they ought to think about it. They talked about whether you'd file charges. Simmons said go ahead right now."

Bradley closed his eyes a moment, trying to cope with it. He had expected anger and threats, but not something quite this drastic.

"Judge, what do they expect to do with a hearing in the

morning? I mean, what can they say that they haven't said already?"

"Public hearing."

"Public!"

"Yep. Already announced it to the loafers out front. Be all over town pretty quick, I reckon. Charging you with misuse of lawful authority, unlawful arrest, withholding evidence, malfeasance in public office—I swan. I never heard so many high-falutin' words." The judge's face turned somber. "You're in bad trouble, Jim."

"Can they do all of that under the town ordinances?"

"I reckon. They wrote the ordinances, you know. Pretty broad powers, there."

"Don't I get some time to file charges? Wrap this up?"

"I'd say you've got till ten o'clock in the morning."

Bradley imagined it. "They'll ask all the same questions. If I don't cave in to them—"

"Might be beyond that, anyways, Jim. Bailey hesitated awhile, but then he joined right in. All the votes was three-zero, except the one to ask Luke Ball to draw up a petition askin' me to issue a search warrant."

Bradley's chair went over as he got to his feet. "A search warrant?"

"Right."

"For what?"

"This office. Your house."

"*Why?*"

"Malfeasance covers a lot of sod, boy. Simmons urged it on, Strider went with him."

"What the hell do they want to search this office or my house for?"

"Don't know. Maybe they're just mad. But it's there in the law books clear as glass. Public official is accused of malfeasance or withholding bona fide evidence, the court can issue search warrants to satisfy the need for valid evidence."

Bradley was stunned. He had expected reaction, but this was all-out war.

"A public hearing," he muttered.

"Correct."

"And a search warrant!"

"Luke is over to his office drawing up the petition. I figger he'll be up in my office another thirty minutes. Do you want to come up and answer the petition?"

"What good will it do me?"

"None," the judge said matter-of-factly. "Law's clear. Warrant will issue."

"Who will do the searching?"

"Good question, being as how you're the lawful authority, at least until they can remove you. I'd guess the court will have to appoint somebody. I'd guess I'll appoint Luke himself."

Bradley rubbed his hands over his face. He reached down and righted the overturned chair, then searched around for his pipe. He found it under some of the papers on the desk. He packed shag tobacco in. His hands trembled slightly.

"So Luke Ball will be down here searching my office in a little while," he said, his voice also betraying the anger.

"That's the law."

Bradley touched a match to the pipe tobacco. He sucked the smoke in. He was having trouble adjusting to this. He saw that he might have made a grievous—even fatal—tactical error. He had assumed an advantage would be his if he hit back unexpectedly. But had he been mousetrapped? Had they assumed from the start that he would hit back . . . *had they outguessed him so that now he had played precisely into their hands?*

It was a harrowing thought. He hated the looks of it.

He asked, "Is there anything I can do legally to stall this off?"

"Don't know of a thing," the old judge said dryly.

Bradley puffed furiously on the pipe.

Judge Johnson waited a minute or two, shrugged, turned, and walked out. The cool night wind made the door slam. The office was silent.

Then a voice came from the cellblock: "Jim Bradley?"

It was Yeager. Bradley had almost forgotten him for a minute.

Still a little dazed, he walked into the dim cellblock where the lantern cast its feeble glow down the rows of bars.

In the end cell, Yeager lay stretched out on the steel cot, his arms behind his head. His teeth showed in a grin as Bradley faced him through the barred door.

"You had me going there for a while," Yeager said.

Bradley didn't say anything.

"You surely did," Yeager crooned. "But I heard that, what was just said out there."

Too late, Bradley saw.

"I don't guess I'm the one that needs to be worrying after all," Yeager told him. "Looks to me like I'll be out of here about ten-thirty tomorrow morning and *you'll* be the one either in here in my place, or packing to go back to Kansas. Yes, sir."

Bradley tried to bluff, although he had no hole card. "You can still save yourself a lot of woe by coming out with the story."

Yeager chuckled, hugely amused. "How about another cup of coffee, Marshal? If you can't send your nigger, just go get it yourself, while good old Luke is searching your office for malfeasance."

TEN

Many of the men who belonged to the farmers' co-operative had brought older sons, so that the crowd assembled under flickering torches beside Phil Schmitz's barn totaled more than fifty. The torches and a few lanterns cast yellowish light that threw gargoyle shadows across the face of the gray barn, the undersides of the trees, and the house a few yards away. Back in the dark were wagons and tied saddle horses.

The mood of the crowd was sullen, angry.

Standing on a crate, Phil Schmitz raised his voice to be heard over the muttering. "The money, it was found. Your payments have been made to the land company. This is the big thing, eh?"

"We want to know what happened," a voice sang out. Others murmured agreement.

His face glistening with sweat despite the cool night air, Schmitz raised his hand for silence. "We have told you."

Dremmerton, the perennial troublemaker, was in the front line. He called out, "Where was it found?"

Watching Schmitz and seeing his instant's pause, John McCollum felt for his friend. They were tied by their pledge to Jim Bradley. Now, with the rumor so widespread, it was not only futile but damaging to continue the sham. But he knew that Schmitz would honor his word.

"The marshal will announce," Schmitz said.

A dissatisfied mutter ran through the crowd.

Dremmerton said, "If it was found on your place, or Mc-Collum's, we got a right to know. And we want to know *why*."

Another man called, "He's got Yeager in jail. That's fine with most of us. Yeager is no friend of ours. But if Yeager took it, how come no charges has been filed?"

"The money is back," Schmitz said. "Safe. Our debts have been paid up to date. That is the important thing."

Wills, Dremmerton's ally, was back in the crowd somewhere but McCollum recognized his reedy voice: "How do we know it won't happen again?"

"*Ach,*" Schmitz grunted. "We cannot guarantee against crime!"

"If it had been in the big vault it wouldn't of happened!" a new voice said.

"The co-operative voted to keep its own records—"

Another man: "Some of us don't like the way this thing smells."

"Wait a minute! Wait a minute," someone else said loudly. "Phil's right. We've got our money back. Our bills is paid. What are we yelling about?"

"We're yelling," someone yelled, "because maybe this money was almost got away with!"

"Phil and John didn't have anything to do with that."

"That's right," another farmer named Stone said. "Just because they're our elected officials, we can't blame them—"

"Not unless they had something to do with it!"

Voices sang out atop one another.

"Are you saying they *stole* the—"

"It was carelessness, we need a regular bookkeeper—"

"I heard the money was right in—"

"We've been doing fine up till now, and just because one bad thing—"

"Wait!" Schmitz pleaded. "Wait!"

Dremmerton bawled, "A lot of us just don't like the way things has been going, is all. Nobody is making any accusations. We just don't like the whole setup."

"What would you do?" Schmitz asked with great, grave dignity. "End the co-operative?"

"Maybe," someone called from the back, "it's time for that!" A few others muttered agreement.

"We've got our debts caught up," a man said. "We've had rain. We got through the crisis. We can't have another bad drought year next year, too. I say maybe the co-op has served its purpose and it's time for us to go back to being free American farmers again."

"No!" someone else yelled.

Dremmerton moved closer to Schmitz's crate and turned to hold up his arms, asking for recognition. "I'm not saying we ought to disband. No, sir. But I'm saying we're at the time where maybe we ought to reorganize. We've growed. We've made money. Times change. People are expressing doubts about our leaders. I'm not saying I doubt anybody. I don't say that at all. But maybe it's time for a vote, here."

"And some of us say forget the whole thing!" someone yelled.

"That's right!"

"I agree with that!"

Phil Schmitz shot McCollum a despairing look, and McCollum knew he had to take a hand. He climbed up on the crate beside his old friend. He had to signal and wait patiently while the babble of voices finally subsided.

He felt the pressure as he spoke, hearing his own voice carry. The men paid attention because he spoke so seldom in these meetings despite his role as cochairman.

"Last summer we had a drought," he began. "Some of you have been here longer than I have and you know how many years there is just such a drought up here in the north part of the canyon. We don't have the springs and spring-fed creeks like they have in the south part. It wasn't raining and our plants were dying in the fields.

"Then we got the idea for hauling water. We got together. For the first time, we all got together. We fixed wagons and we set up schedules. We went to Low Point on the river and got the water.

"You remember the fight we had over the right to haul water from Low Point. We wouldn't have gotten through that —we wouldn't have gotten the water and we couldn't have hauled it to our fields—unless we worked together. And I think since some of you have been talking about Jim Bradley here earlier tonight, and wondering about him, you ought to try to remember that it was Jim Bradley who faced down those people who wanted to stop us from getting the water."

"That was last summer," someone yelled.

"Let me finish," McCollum yelled back as his anger got away.

The man shut up.

"Each of us is better off today than we would have been without the co-operative," McCollum resumed. "Some of us, myself included, probably wouldn't still be here if we hadn't gotten together.

"Now we've had some trouble. We don't know exactly what happened. Stories are flying around that make Phil look bad, and me look bad. Some of you doubt us. That's your right. But let me ask this: *Don't kill the co-op*. It was formed in trouble and it can't be allowed to die the first time it faces some new trouble. Do you doubt Phil and me? All right. Have an election. Pick new chairmen. Reorganize. But don't stop working together, because alone none of us has a chance!"

He stopped, his voice having reached a crescendo.

There was a moment's total silence.

"He's right," someone said. "We can't break up now."

"Yeah, but we can't go on this way, neither!"

"Then let's have us a new election!"

"Here and now?"

"Here and now."

"These guys have done all right by us. I say let things go as they have."

"If the majority wants a new election, have it!"

"For me, I'm sick of my money going into a box somewheres where I can't even git at it, and then somebody makes off with it and I don't know what's going on."

"Vote, then!"

Voices clamored. "Vote!"

"Is that what you want?" McCollum asked. "A vote?"

They yelled affirmatively, with only a few dissents.

"How do you want to vote?"

Dremmerton said, "I say we vote on whether to continue. That's first."

McCollum glanced at Schmitz. He saw the same awareness in his friend's eyes. They were going to ballot this casually on their future. But there was nothing to do about it. The majority had always ruled, and in the general excitement there could be no doubt that the men wanted the vote.

"All right," McCollum said, and instantly it was quieter than it had been all evening. "All those in favor of continuing the co-op, say 'aye.'"

"Aye!" voices roared.

"Those who want to quit, say 'nay.'"

A much weaker chorus sang out.

Over the hubbub McCollum said, "The vote is to continue."

"Mr. Chairman!" It was Dremmerton.

"Yes?"

"I think now we have to have another vote. On whether we want to change chairmen."

"Leave them alone!" someone yelled angrily.

"No!" another man called back. "He's right. We got a right!"

Arguments started spontaneously everywhere.

Schmitz leaned close to McCollum and said into his ear, "This vote. If they vote us down, what then?"

"Then Dremmerton will probably take over," McCollum said.

"How can you be so *calm?* He is not a smart man! He will ruin everything!"

"It's a democracy, Phil. If people want to vote for their own destruction, they have that right, too, you know."

Schmitz rolled his eyes. *"Ach!"*

McCollum held up his hands for attention. "Do you want to vote on this other question?"

"Vote of confidence," someone called, and it was Wills. "Vote 'yes' to keep Schmitz and McCollum, vote 'no' against them. If they lose, we hold a new election."

"Get paper," someone else suggested. "Secret ballot."

Surprisingly, the crowd hushed with these words. They all knew they were going to do it.

McCollum turned to Schmitz and his voice carried despite its low tone. "Can we get some pencils and paper?"

"Ja," Schmitz sighed. "I can fetch it."

As the old German climbed down off the crate and headed for the house, McCollum maintained a calm face as he watched new, restrained arguments begin to break out all through the crowd of men. Some pointed at others, arguing a point, and others smacked a fist into a palm. The voices rumbled. McCollum felt a stab of bitterness, that it would come to this after the work he and Schmitz had put in. This vote, he thought, would not be one-sided like the other had been. This would be close. And maybe Dremmerton, if he won and got control, would have a hollow victory, because it was possible that no one would be able to hold the organization together after the strain of an evenly divided election.

They were, in other words, voting at the worst possible time.

McCollum wondered suddenly if people always did that.

If Yeager had not overheard the conversation about suspension, Jim Bradley thought, things might still have developed according to the fragile plan. But now it was blown out of the water. Bradley was numbed.

Standing in his office, he had spent several minutes in which thought was random, disconnected, and virtually meaningless. It was the worst blow yet and perhaps the fatal one. Now he not only might lose his job, and with it the last chance to solve the mystery, but could carry away with him the kind of disgrace that went ahead of a man, shadowing his life forever.

And yet he had to try to get over the shock. If there was still something he could do, he had to do it.

He couldn't see a hopeful course of action.

He reviewed what the town board planned to do. A suspension hearing was designed to force him at last to come out into the open with what was essentially a ridiculous case, based only on guesses and intuition. Then at best his plan was ruined, and the chances for worse consequences were clear enough.

He could not understand, however, the order for Luke Ball to seek a search warrant. Malfeasance in office? Was that just another way to punish him? What could they even remotely hope to find with some kind of search? Did they think the money would be found? It had *already* been found. What, then? Did they think he was hiding some kind of evidence?

If they assumed he was really protecting his friends, then this might be their motivation. The search warrant, in this event, was a fishing license. They probably would have no idea what they might find, but since they had been told the money had been found almost blindly, perhaps they hoped something else would turn up equally without rational explanation.

Bradley stiffened as he made a connection.

Was there a pattern?

The events so far pivoted upon the inexplicable finding of the loot in McCollum's and Schmitz's possession.

What if the plan was more complex than he had so far anticipated? What if the loot had been planted, but *something more* had been planted? On *him?*

The thought chilled him all over again. He looked around the office. Here? Could someone have hidden something here? His house was more likely. But it could be here. There were the desks. And the small safe.

Even now, judging by the faint sounds of voices through the walls, Luke Ball was next door talking to the judge. He might be here within minutes.

The possibility of planted evidence was real enough, seen with this new perspective, that Bradley knew he had to move fast. He went first to his desk, shuffled through the papers on top. Nothing but his notes, Wanted posters, some old letters. He went through the drawers one at a time, shoveling with his hands. Some pens, ink, charge forms, old payroll vouchers, more posters, more old mail—none of it valuable—some envelopes, extra jail silverware, coffee and sugar and salt, some spent shell casings for reloading, the cabinet keys, a broken spur, his letter of appointment, some maps, a couple of livery bills stamped *paid,* an eraser, a broken pipe and some tobacco, the sack of Yeager's watch and money.

Freddie Smith's desk was even barer. Except for some old posters, a bottle with about two ounces of whiskey in the bottom, and a key chain, Smith's drawers were empty.

There was nothing to be hidden in the gun cabinet. It was wholly open, only the lock and chain through trigger guards holding the weapons in security.

Bradley went to the small safe in the corner and unlocked it. He knelt as he swung the small, stout door back. Shoving the key ring into his pocket, he peered into the dark, cramped interior. Five boxes of ammunition were stacked against the back wall. The petty cash can, containing a few dollars, was also there. That was all.

Except for a folded piece of paper whose corner stuck out of the money can. He would not have noticed it unless he had been looking extra sharply.

He did not recognize it.

Pulling it out, he unfolded it. It was a note, written in pencil. His skin crawled as he read it.

JIM

WE GOT IT FINE. FOLLOW PLAN. NOBODY KNOWS HOW MUCH TOTAL. YOU'LL GET YOUR SHARE AFTER FOLKS CALM DOWN.

JOHN

Instinctively Bradley crumpled the note and shoved it into his pocket with the keys. His first impulse was to get the thing out of sight because of how incriminating it could be.

He sat on the floor, staring at the safe.

An outsider would read it only one way, and a fool could make the leaps to fill in the gaps: "John" was McCollum, and he and/or Schmitz had taken the loot with Bradley's help. They had then conspired to return what people *thought* was the total, while the three of them raked off a tidy profit from what the true total had been.

Somebody had planted the note—and someone else on the town board had *known* the note was planted and just waiting for a legal search to uncover it. No one would then listen to protestations that only an idiot would hang on to such incriminating evidence against himself. The rush to convict would be on. Schmitz would be finished. McCollum would be finished. And Emerald Canyon would be looking for a new marshal because the old one would be behind bars.

Sweat trickled down Bradley's face as he saw how damned close it had come to working. If he hadn't connected the pattern of hidden evidence—!

The door opened and he turned on his buttocks, deeply alarmed with the kind of guilt that real criminals felt. He expected Luke Ball.

It was Freddie Smith, his eyes big from the dark, the shotgun in hand. "Everything's fine," he said gently, walking to the gun cabinet.

Bradley got to his feet and tried to get his thoughts and feelings organized. The first thing he had to do was get rid of the note. That might not be good legal action, but he was in a fight for his survival now.

"Been checkin' the safe?" Smith asked with interest, coming over.

"Wanted to see how much ammo we had," Bradley lied.

"Guess we got plenty. We sure haven't had much call to use any."

"Freddie, do you have a key to this safe?"

"No, sir. Only one is the one you got on the ring. Why?"

Bradley felt a little guilty about the suspicion. It showed how upset he was. But *someone* had planted the evidence, and recently.

He said, "Luke Ball and the judge will be around in a little bit. They'll want to look around. You co-operate with them."

"What's going on?"

"They want to check for evidence."

Smith's face drooped. "I see."

"I'll leave you the key. I've got to make a few rounds myself. You can open up for them." Bradley swung the safe door closed and it clicked tightly.

"That's fine," Smith smiled. "But I'll tell you a secret. If they really wanted in that thing, I guess I could oblige 'em without no key."

"What do you mean by that?" Bradley asked sharply.

The black man was amused and relaxed. "Some wore-out safes are funny. Like this one. Not many folks know, but a locksmith showed me once."

"Showed you what?"

Smith put his big hands on the corners of the safe. "Want to help me, please?" He pushed the top of the safe, starting to tilt it so it would lie over on its side. Inside, the boxes of ammunition slid around.

Puzzled, Bradley helped. They laid the little safe on its side. Then Smith grabbed the small, stout legs and lifted, with Bradley's help, setting the safe on its top, upside down.

As they swung it fully upside down, something clicked metallically inside.

The door swung open.

"See," Smith said, amused, "the lock raises or lowers this thick steel bar inside the door. See? It goes up and down to block it so you can't open it. Well, these little older models get wore real bad. You turn it full upside down, the bar slides back of its own weight, and there you are."

"For God's sake," Bradley said.

"Lucky thing, durned few folks know. Safes like this all over the country, the man tole me."

So that part was explained, and Bradley had trouble coping with this latest surprise. Anyone who knew could have come in, inverted the safe to open it, put the incriminating bogus note in the petty cash can.

Anyone who had a chance to be alone in the office in the past day or so.

Which was when he remembered something.

"I remember you saying earlier that this safe is worn out," he said. "Could the *other* safe have a similar defect?"

"The one the money was in?"

"Yes."

"Nope. Different kind of safe. I'm afraid that one won't open for no tricks like we just pulled on this one."

"Let's get this thing right side up again. And when Luke and the judge come down, you co-operate with them fully. But don't tell them about *this* little trick, right?"

Smith nodded, becoming serious again. "This trouble is bad?"

They sweated the safe to its feet. "It's bad, Freddie. But maybe I see a glimmer of light. I've got to go out for a little while. You watch the office."

"Yes, sir."

Leaving the keys but making sure the note was still in his pocket, Bradley hurriedly left the office. The night was cool and windy, with the rain still holding off. He saw no one on the street. He walked quickly away from the City Building because he did not want to be stopped now.

Bing had been in the office alone when he got there earlier. He was absolutely sure in his own mind that Bing had somehow known the trick with the safe and had planted the false evidence. He remembered now for the first time that there had been a film of sweat on the foreman's face, as if he had just been going through strenuous exertion or strong emotion. Inverting the heavy little safe alone, and in a hurry while fearing apprehension, would provide plenty of both.

And Bing worked for Samuel Kane.

The puzzle began to fall into place.

Still walking, Bradley bit his lips as he realized, however, that what he knew and what he could prove were vastly different things. He had nothing to go on, and was now in even worse shape than that because he had the bogus note that self-preservation demanded he destroy.

The thing to do, he thought, was bury it. Or burn it. Or throw it down a well or something like that, a place no one would ever look.

And then he stopped dead in the middle of the street and smacked his palm against his forehead because it had just truly clicked for him. On the heels of the other realization about Bing, he remembered the other thing that he had overlooked right from the start.

It gave him the knowledge of exactly what he had to do, and with some luck—my God!—with some luck, he could have his evidence.

He hurried back toward the jail to get what he needed.

In the torchlit clearing near the Schmitz barn, the ballots had been cast, each slip of paper tossed in a brown paper sack as the men filed by the packing-crate podium. Now two farmers were counting under the light of lanterns held aloft by Schmitz and the nervous Dremmerton. Some men stood

nearby, clustering to hear the Yeses and Noes droned out.
Others milled around talking excitedly. John McCollum had
drifted to the edge of the crowd nearest the house, and stood
leaning against the gnarled trunk of an old apple tree. He
was in darkness and alone.

Or so he thought.

A voice behind him asked quietly, "You do not help
count?"

McCollum turned sharply and recognized Phil Schmitz's
wife standing there in the gloom. A big woman with a face
that was ordinarily pink and in glowing good humor in spite
of hardships, she was hardly more than a shadow in the dark.

"You've been listening?" McCollum countered, realizing
that he should not be surprised.

"*Ja,*" Mrs. Schmitz replied softly. "This thing, I know what
it means to my husband."

"To a lot of us," McCollum agreed.

"I do not understand these men. Why must stealing of the
money be the fault of my husband? Or of you?"

"They don't all feel that way," McCollum said, aware of
the hollow sound of his own voice.

"But you do not watch the counting of votes."

"No."

"Why?"

"I don't know. I must be tired."

"But you care."

"Of course." A thought struck him. "I think I care too much
to want to watch the counting. The totals go this way and
that way, and it takes too much out of a man to watch it. I'll
know the final tally soon enough."

"My husband, if you lose the vote, will see it as disgrace.
You will be the same?"

"I don't know," McCollum repeated wearily. "It won't make
sense to view it that way. Elected officials win and lose. The
voting isn't always right. If we lose, then someone else has to
take charge. It will give Phil and me more time for our own

work and our own families. God knows I've wanted more time. . . ."

"Your wife, she is almost due now."

"Yes. Maybe losing the vote would be the best thing. Then I could be with her more. We wouldn't have to meet at night, go over the books, write letters and send telegrams trying to find the best markets, visit men to arrange wagons and crews, set up water-shipment quotas, go around talking, talking—" McCollum took a sharp breath. "I'm awfully tired of meetings, and talking!"

Mrs. Schmitz was silent for a while. Across the clearing, the counting went on. They were nearing the end.

Finally she said, "But you want to continue being leader. Like my husband."

"Only if the men want me."

"But you want it."

"Yes."

"Why? They accuse you of things. They, how do you say, drag foots. Make life harder for you."

"We've built something here. We have to fight for it. We have to stand together. I want to do my part."

"If you lose? Then what?"

McCollum surveyed the prospect. "Then I'll try to help the new man."

"Even Dremmerton? Who wants only glory?"

"It doesn't matter what a man's motives are. Our working together: *that's* what's important."

"I think you are good man," Mrs. Schmitz said slowly after another pause. "I think you like my Phil. I think you work for others, even if others do not pay you back."

"All of us came here to try to have good lives, Mrs. Schmitz. We're working for that together. If they turn your husband and me down, what we have to do is say it's somehow for the better—we have to keep trying, because we can only make it together."

"But you lose, you hurt. Bad."

"Yes," McCollum admitted, and in the single word he felt the intensity of his feelings.

The bulky woman's hand touched his arm. "You are good man. I go back inside now. Watch from window. A woman's place is not in a meeting like this, eh? Someday, women can vote. But not yet. Not in my time."

At the packing crate, the lanterns moved suddenly, being readjusted, sending shots of geometric pattern against the barn and undersides of tree leaves.

"Vote's in!" someone called.

The woman faded into the dark. McCollum turned and walked briskly around the edge of the crowd toward the crate. Phil Schmitz was already climbing up on it, and before a word was said, McCollum knew by the flush on his friend's face and the way Dremmerton, his lips pulled back in a bitter scowl, walked toward his former place in the crowd.

"The vote," Schmitz said, and the crowd fell silent, "is this. *Yes,* to keep present officers, twenty-five. *No,* to have new election, fourteen. Others"—but here the roar drowned out his words except for those close to him, like McCollum, who just managed to hear him add—"did not vote."

Schmitz turned and looked down at McCollum. His face was streaming sweat and his eyes glinted with victory. He started to say something.

At that moment, however, there was a new commotion at the back of the crowd. Men pulled away, making way for someone, and McCollum saw that a horseman—a south end farmer whose name he didn't remember—was riding excitedly right up to the packing crate. Men yelled at him, and he waved his arms for silence.

"Town board just met!" he announced. "They're gonna meet again in the morning, maybe fire Jim Bradley! They're searching his office right now and people say he's *gonna* be fired at the meeting in the morning!"

The first drops of rain spattered down, making sharp, hissing noises in the torches.

Walking quietly through the alley with the coiled rope over his shoulder, Jim Bradley felt every sense begin to work overtime as he tried to pick out any slightest sound or sight that could indicate the presence of another human. The alley was black, deserted. Raindrops patted warmly on his back and shoulders. He could hear voices on the street a half block away, but the alley was utterly silent.

Bradley's feet felt light without his customary riding boots. The thin-soled, low-cut moccasins picked out every pebble underfoot and gave him a decidedly odd sensation. But they were perfect for the task to be undertaken.

When he reached the broader alley area roughly behind the Simmons Feed and Produce Company, he backed against the board wall and stood quiet for several minutes, allowing his eyes further time to adjust to the dark while he scrutinized every doorway and window that faced the area. He saw no lights and no movement.

This was dangerous in a way that he could not wholly predict. His belly was tight. But he moved away from the wall without hesitation once he had satisfied himself that no other human was around at the moment. He went directly to the abandoned water well in the middle of the dirt area, stepping lightly over some trash that careless hands had tossed at the opening, missing.

The old well had a circular opening about five feet in diameter. A rock wall extended upward from ground level about four feet. Some of the rocks had fallen but the wall was still well defined. There was also, buried deeply in the ground at one end, a length of thick rusty pipe that had once supported the overhead pulley for the bucket draw apparatus.

Uncoiling his rope, Bradley snubbed one end firmly around the rusty pipe, then circled it once around and under a large rock that lay nearby. He took the remainder of the rope and tossed it over the round wall, letting it uncoil inside the well shaft. It made dry, rustling sounds going down. Like a rat or a snake.

There might be both down in the well, he thought, but then forced himself to ignore the possibility.

With another look around, he put a leg over the rock wall and sat on the edge. He grabbed the rope, testing its tie to the steel post. It felt firm.

He lowered himself over the edge, supporting his total weight by his grasp on the rope. He started down into blackness that made the alley seem like daylight.

The walls of the well inside were uneven, patched here and there with moss and spider webs. He couldn't see a thing. A musty odor came up from the depths, sharply assailing his nostrils. He tried to breathe deeply now despite the odor because he knew it would get worse as he went down. The rope began to burn his hands, and his thick shoulder muscles sent knifelike pain messages to his brain.

It was about forty feet, he knew, to the water table. But the well had gone bad—seepage from nearby sources of pollution—quite some time ago, and in the intervening years it had been a place to dump trash. Going down hand over hand, using his soft-soled shoes to help purchase holds on the rough rock sidewalls, Bradley hoped to reach the top level of debris and sediment at about the fifteen-foot level.

At fifteen feet the stench was really getting bad, but his feet had not reached bottom. He let himself down deeper, slowing his descent as old fears of depths and closed places began to assail him despite all his intentions and resolutions to the contrary.

He had been seven or eight years old when he first found out about closed places and the fear they could bring out in him. He was in an old house on the edge of St. Louis with his older brother, Victor. He could still remember everything with the vivid clarity of childhood: the rotted smells of the old house, the high windows that looked out onto elms that shrouded the walls, the holes in the roof of the second-floor bedroom where something had broken the structure fatally, sending its occupants elsewhere to leave it as a ghost that invited animals and children out for a spooky place to play.

He and Victor had been in the back bedroom, the one with the narrow staircase that went down to what had once been a kitchen. It was their favorite place for playing spooks or hide-and-seek. Bradley was "it," and he turned his face to the wall to hide his eyes while Victor ran out of sight somewhere.

"You're peeking!" Victor claimed.

"No! I ain't!"

"Are too!"

"Am not!"

"Aw right, then, get in that closet, there, and close the door! Then you *can't* peek!"

"Don't need to!"

"You're scared!"

"I'll show you I ain't scared, dummy!" And he bolted into the closet.

The door slammed—latched.

He was in blackness, closed in tightly, dust flying in his nostrils and his hands banging on rough wood and mildewed wallpaper, and he couldn't see a thing—knew he was already out of air.

"Victor! *Victor! Let me out!*"

Nothing.

His hands found the door latch inside, but it was rusty and stuck. He hurled his weight against the door but it would not give. The dark rushed in and he started screaming, knowing he was out of air, knowing he was going to die, going crazy to be out.

Then, suddenly, the door swung wide and there was Victor grinning at him, and the blessed light and air of the room.

"What's the matter, dummy? Can't you take a joke?"

But that moment was one that had always remained with Bradley. Now, going deeper into the well, he felt the same child within him, trying to break loose and take control and *lose* control, screaming and sobbing with no reason.

There was plenty of air, he reassured himself. His danger was not from lack of air, or from being trapped. He had the rope. The danger was that someone might discover him—someone who should not discover him and would see what he was really after.

But he had to ignore that, too.

He went down another ten feet or so. His left foot, extended below to feel bottom, touched something papery that rustled. He stopped his descent and hung from the rope while he felt around some more with his toes. A bottle clinked and some tin cans rustled against more paper or cardboard.

Lashing the rope twice around his chest and under his armpits, he braced his feet against the side and hung in his makeshift harness while he got a stub of candle and matches from his vest pocket. He struck a match on the rock sidewall, but it was too wet from drainage and the match wouldn't strike. He cracked another match on his thumb. The light flared, smoking yellowly, and he touched it to the candle. The wick caught and flickered, moving around wildly in an eerie little draft whose origin he could not guess.

The candlelight seemed very bright in the hole. He saw spiders rushing around on the rocks, trying to get away. Beneath his braced feet was a clutter of cardboard, papers, cans, bottles, pieces of wooden crates, and bursted paper bags of garbage. The stuff was compacted only loosely from its fall down the shaft and he knew it would not bear his weight. The whole mess might plunge down several feet if he tried to stand on it.

Readjusting his rope harness, he lowered himself until his buttocks almost rested on the trash. Then he found a chink in the rocks of the wall and jammed the candle in so that it stuck out, burning, like a miniature torch. This freed his hands and he could hang over in his harness, the blood rushing uncomfortably to his head. He carefully moved some of the tin cans to one side, sifted with his fingers in the paper and ashes beneath them, then moved the cans back in place and shifted a piece of crate slightly.

Beneath the top layers of trash, things moved around and broke loose, and he heard chunks of stuff plopping into water far below. Panic tried to take over as he felt himself falling the depth of the shaft into water beyond the end of the rope, but this lasted only a second before he got control of himself again. The trash plug in the well had not entirely fallen; its surface had shifted only slightly. He had to be more careful but he could still hope.

The ropes cut him painfully. His half-inverted position made his head feel like it was going to explode. He could feel the veins standing out. He forced his concentration to center on his fingertips as he kept sifting.

With a forced, meticulous care he went over the top layer of rubbish. Then he raised himself upright and leaned more weight against the sidewall and breathed normally for a few minutes. He noticed that the candle stub was half gone already, burning faster than normally because of its side position. He lowered himself again, hanging in the ropes to sift deeper with his fingers.

He was due a little luck, he told himself. Maybe it had been his own stupidity, not seeing the pattern earlier. He had suspected that some of the events of that night earlier had been part of some pattern, and then he had become convinced that it all focused on the savings and loan break-in. But then he had gotten so preoccupied with the mystery of the safe itself, and the finding of the loot, that he hadn't reconstructed carefully enough.

He still had only this theory. But he knew it was correct. Now he needed the luck.

Sometimes luck was helped along if you worked hard enough. His arms going dead from painful lack of circulation, he kept probing.

It was more than thirty minutes later that Freddie Smith, alone again in the jail office after the judge and Luke Ball had come and searched, looked up at the sound from the door and was startled to see his boss enter.

"Land!" Smith gasped.

Bradley was covered with mud, moss, spider webs, soot, garbage, and other stuff that Smith could not even begin to speculate on. But he came across the room like a freight train, dropped into his desk chair, grabbed out some paper and a pen and ink, and started scribbling without even washing his hands first.

"Were they here?" he asked, not pausing as the words on the paper flowed out in a neat hand.

"Yes, sir," Smith said, a little awed.

"Out at my house now, I suppose?"

"They said so—"

"Freddie, I've got a job for you. It's a long ride, but you've got to leave for the county seat."

"*Now?*" Smith breathed, even more astonished.

"Right now," Bradley said. "I've got letters for you to deliver. You've got to get them delivered tonight."

"It'll be plumb in the middle of the night before I can git there!"

"It will be almost morning," Bradley agreed, still forcing the words onto paper. "Go get one of our fast horses. Diamond Face. He's fastest. And push him all the way. You've got to get there so these people can be back here before noon tomorrow."

"Diamond Face don't go distances," Freddie protested. "It'll hurt him."

"You won't have to ride him back. You can leave him there and come back on a rent horse."

"Against town rules to rent horses off like that," Freddie pointed out.

Bradley looked up for just an instant, his eyes showing a keen anxiety that was mixed with something else, some form of pleasure or anticipation.

"That's the least of our worries right now, Freddie," he said. "Go get the horse. I'll have these letters written by the time you get back here, ready to go. Hurry."

ELEVEN

The pealing of the church bell startled Bradley out of restive sleep. Sitting up on the cot in the corner of the jail office, he remembered everything instantly and also realized that it was Sunday. But it would be no ordinary Sunday.

His pocket watch showed eight o'clock. He hadn't been able to sleep after getting Freddie Smith off on his trip; it had been almost four when sleep finally came. Now Bradley felt numbed, stiff, creaky, old-mannish in the joints.

Pulling on his trousers, he limped outside to the well in the side yard of the City Building and hauled up a metal cylinder of water. The rainstorm had passed through in the night, leaving brilliantly blue sky and cool air that would heat as the day wore on. Bradley poured the container of water into his porcelain bucket and carried it back into the office, where he washed and shaved, cutting himself on the upper lip.

The food cabinet in the cellblock corridor contained some cans of tomatoes and beans and a few biscuits hard enough to break rocks. He took a couple of cans and the biscuits and utensils into the office and got some wood burning in the stove. He put coffee on in the white pot and dumped a can of tomatoes and one of beans into a pan, also putting them on to heat.

The stove and the sun began to heat the building as he went back deeper into the cellblock to H. R. Yeager's cell. Yeager, puffy-faced and rumpled, sat on the edge of the steel cot. He didn't say anything as Bradley collected the slop pail, re-locked the door, and left to take it out back. On his return Bradley took Yeager a basin of water, a washcloth, and a towel.

"How about soap?" Yeager asked.

"Out. Sorry."

Yeager's lips turned derisively but he didn't comment. He was still in his hardcase act after hearing last night's conversations and the search.

Going into his office again, Bradley stirred the breakfast concoction. The stove had heated a bright pink and the coffee was boiling. He poured out mugs of the stuff and dumped the tomatoes and beans into two tin plates. Putting a couple of the rocky biscuits on the edge of one plate, he carried it back to Yeager's cell and slid the plate and coffee mug under the door.

Yeager looked and turned up his nose. "Am I supposed to eat that?"

"You can eat it or stick it in your ear," Bradley snapped.

"Testy today, Jim?"

Bradley started to turn away.

"Since you took my watch," Yeager added, "I can't tell exactly what time it is. But the bell starts at eight. That was quite a while ago. Church is at nine. Almost nine by now? That means we don't have much more than an hour before the meeting next door, right?"

"You're chipper enough," Bradley observed.

"You've been high-handed since the day you got to Emerald Canyon. I'm going to enjoy watching you get your comeuppance."

"Don't be too sure."

"I'm sure. You don't have a leg to stand on. You went too far this time, arresting law-abiding citizens—"

"Don't talk to me about law-abiding!" Bradley flared. "You bastards have had it your own way around here since the Year One. You've had the land, the money, the loan business, the law—everything. You haven't obeyed the law; you've made the law fit your ideas of what it ought to be."

Yeager smiled. "Save your speeches for the hearing. You'll need them."

Bradley walked out. Shaky-mad, he sat at his desk and tried to eat. He couldn't get anything solid down. The coffee was putrid, as his coffee generally was. He had gotten pretty spoiled on Jean Reff's coffee, he thought, which made him remember the way he had backed away from her last night, which further depressed him.

He was not sure why he had done that. But he had always backed off from other people in crisis. A man had to stand alone. He could not fight anything or anyone with the tin cans of devotion clanging and banging from long threads tied around his neck. But it was *lonely*. He saw that now.

His watch showed almost nine. He left the office and walked out front, remaining in the shadow of the City Building. Men, women, and children streamed up the street, some afoot and others in carriages, headed for the church. A few of them saw him, fewer waved; most looked away as quickly as they spotted his figure in the shadows. They looked curiously embarrassed. They didn't know how to act toward him now. They probably didn't know what to think, either.

The front door of the City Building opened. Henry Strider, T. L. Bailey, and Luke Ball came out. Then came Thomas S. Simmons and old Judge Johnson, and finally, a little to Bradley's surprise, came Samuel Kane. So there had been a grand strategy meeting just before church, getting ready for the public session at ten. And Sam Kane was now an open part of things.

On the surface, this would appear natural to bystanders. Kane had opened the canyon to white settlement, stealing, terrorizing, and/or cheating the earlier white owners out of the entire area. Using his immense wealth, won on cattle drives, he had built Emerald Canyon in his image and then retired to the finest corner of it, seemingly remote from everyday affairs of the town and poorer folk.

Bradley knew better. During the crisis over water rights, immediately after his arrival earlier in the summer, he had discovered plenty of evidence of Kane's business tie-ins with members of the town board and others along Main Street. Kane was the power and the brains behind everything important that happened. His appearance here now proved how close to the center of things he was on this situation. But of course Bradley had already known that.

As the men went down the building steps to the street, one or the other spotted Bradley and said something. The others turned their heads as one. Kane's lips turned in a slight smile and he raised his hand in a half salute. Bradley did not respond and they walked down the street toward the church.

Knowing that the telegraph office would be open by now, Bradley headed in the opposite direction. He had little hope on the wire he had sent to the safe company, but it never hurt to try. He found old Jed Dozier sleepily on duty at the silent key, but yes, Jed said, there was a wire, came in a little while ago. He handed it over.

The safe company said it had no record of inquiry or key duplication on the safe whose serial numbers Bradley had sent.

So much for that.

Bradley headed back for the jail. The church bell had stopped. The street was empty except for him, and the wind was still for once, so that the morning had a crystal quality which cleared the air and seemed to magnify the warped boards of storefronts. He turned and looked up the street toward the point where it bent to leave town and head south, into the country, headed for the south pass and the road to the county seat. There was no one.

The cramped interior of the sod house was all hustle and bustle. John McCollum had been up early to do some chores and fix breakfast, but naturally Mrs. Schmitz and Mrs. Wimberley had brought what seemed a ton of food with them, and they were cooking all over again. Mary McCollum sat at the table sipping a fresh cup of coffee and chattering with the women about some of those things that men never fully understand.

Going back in, McCollum removed his hat to lean over and kiss his wife on the cheek. His face, she thought, looked pale and drawn. She hid her concern.

"I'll be back in a few hours," he told her.

Mrs. Wimberley turned and put fists on her wide hips. "Just so you bring us back good news!"

McCollum smiled thinly. "We'll do our best."

"Be careful," Mary McCollum told him.

He kissed her lightly again and left the dugout, allowing the door to swing ajar onto the sun-filled entrance. Mary McCollum heard his voice outside, then the replies of the other two men, and then there was the sound of horses and saddle leather and movement and they were gone.

"I hope it comes out all right," Mrs. Schmitz said stoically.

"It has to," Mrs. Wimberley replied. "I swan! What could they do to a man like Jim Bradley?"

The two women began talking about it, but Mary McCollum did not take part. She was so worried. Although she was supposed to be a simple ninny, and not know what was going on, she still had a friend or two who gave her credit for good sense. She knew how the money had vanished and how it had been found—and where. She probably knew as much or more about today's hearing than either of the other wives did. She also knew the pressure her husband was under, and what this could mean to their future.

If Jim Bradley fell, she thought, it was the beginning of a backward slide to the way things had been before he arrived. Oh, the co-operative had been a splendid idea, the men had worked hard together, they had had some good luck, and some people in other parts of the canyon had changed attitudes, become more friendly. But Jim Bradley had been the start of all the change for the better; he was the single man who stood between the co-op, the individuals, the poor, on the one hand, and people like Henry Strider and his land company.

If Bradley fell, she knew, the land payment crises would accelerate again. New water rights problems would be raised. The pressure would be on, and some other marshal would come, docile at the whim of the town board, to serve papers, then evict.

Some of the others might think Jim Bradley's crisis today was one affecting a powerful friend. But Mary McCollum saw clearly that it was a crisis that meant the future of all of them. He was their rock. Their lives—the life of this child stirring within her right now—depended very directly on what happened in that meeting today.

And she was frightened.

When church services ended, a bit earlier than usual at ten minutes before ten, Sam Kane stood near the front steps with the preacher and some friends and nodded and smiled expansively and tipped his hat to the folks. His mind was entirely upon the meeting that was about to start, but he had to hide the intensity of his feelings because he was, after all, a public figure.

A man from the livery barn named Archington, a little fellow with a bad leg, as all liverymen seemed to have from lives with recalcitrant and sometimes dangerous animals, scurried up behind Kane and plucked at his sleeve for attention.

"Mr. Kane!"

"Hello, Mrs. Brewster!" Kane beamed, doffing his hat again. "Not now, Henry."

"It's important!" Archington whispered.

Irritated, Kane half-turned.

Archington was sweaty with excitement. "The sheriff is in town."

"Harding?"

"Yes, sir. And the county attorney, Windle. Him, too."

Kane saw the frown of surprise on the faces of Strider and Bailey, who stood on either side of him and had overheard. "Where are they?"

"With Marshal Bradley."

"Where?"

"In his office."

Kane spotted another familiar face and beamed at it. "Morning, Mr. Sloan! Nice service! Yes!" He turned and signaled his associates and they drifted down the plank sidewalk a safe distance away to huddle.

"What are they here for?" Strider asked. He was red-faced from a celluloid collar that seemed too tight.

"Bradley sent for them," Kane said. "What else?"

"Why?" Simmons grunted.

"I don't know," Kane admitted.

"If he has something up his sleeve—"

"What could he have up his sleeve?" Kane thought about it and relaxed. "If he thinks having county officials here will help, he's farther gone than I thought. Fact is, I wish I had thought of that myself. Gives the proceedings more authority and class, having county folks here. Wouldn't you agree?"

His associates, of course, agreed. The crowd was drifting toward the City Building. It was almost ten.

Jim Bradley waited a full two minutes after Sheriff Harding and County Attorney Windle left his office before he started for the door to go to the town board's open meeting. He pulled the door of the office open abruptly and almost bumped into Jean Reff.

"Oh!" she said, startled. Her hand had been raised to knock. She looked pretty in a Sunday church dress, a pale lavender with a matching bonnet that framed her face with embroidery work.

Bradley was so glad to see her that he blurted immediately, "Look. I'm sorry about last night."

"I came to say almost the same thing."

"It was my fault. I didn't have to be rude."

"I pried."

"No."

They looked at each other and he wanted to take her in his arms.

Instead, he said, "I guess the meeting is about to start."

"Yes," she said.

They walked around the building together, close but not touching except as the folds of her full skirt brushed against his leg. She was not just pretty, Bradley thought; she was downright beautiful. He felt proud to have her beside him.

They reached the front of the building. The crowd had spilled out onto the steps and into the street. The murmuring ceased as Bradley, taking Jean's hand, led her up the stairs and through the crowd inside.

TWELVE

Intense heat from the packed crowd enveloped Bradley as he led Jean Reff into the meeting room. Every chair was taken and men lined the walls up the sides and along the back. Sunlight flooded into the room through the high side windows, making cigar smoke blue. At the front, the members of the town board were already behind the table, and Bradley spotted Judge Johnson and Luke Ball seated off the ends of the table. There were some men standing near the flanking flags whom he supposed had been appointed as informal bailiffs. Conversations roared.

Jean pulled her hand out of his. "I'll stand back here."

"No," Bradley told her. "Come on."

"I can stand back here."

"I want you with me."

Her eyes changed for a split second. "Do you?"

"Please." The unfamiliar word felt strange on his tongue.

They made their way up the narrow aisle between the rows of chairs. As they reached the front, he saw that several empty chairs had been arranged along one wall. He walked with Jean to two of them nearest the board table and they sat down.

Henry Strider was seated at the center chair at the board table. Thomas Simmons was on his right, the far side from where Bradley was, and T. L. Bailey was on his left. All three men wore their Sunday suits despite the heat that made sweat stream down their faces. They looked uncomfortable, and while Strider and Simmons appeared grimly set on the task at hand, Bailey also appeared nervous: he kept fidgeting with the papers that lay on the nearly empty table in front of him.

With a glance toward Bradley and a side word to his fellow members, Henry Strider picked up a small gavel and began rapping it on the table. Conversation in the room began to dwindle, but some people didn't hear.

"Order, please," Strider said. He banged again.

The room stilled, so that the sound of flies buzzing on the ceiling was suddenly loud by contrast.

"The town board of Emerald Canyon will come to order," Strider said. "Special meeting, called by vote of this board after executive session held in this same room last night." He glanced toward Luke Ball, who had scribbled a note on a long pad. "The record should show the board is present, and also the town attorney, Mr. Luke Ball, and municipal Judge J. J. Johnson. Marshal Jim Bradley is present. Meeting is open meeting with citizens present."

Strider paused, swept his slightly bulging eyes around the room, allowed himself a slight smile. "Gentlemen"—a glance toward Jean Reff—"and ladies. The board apologizes for having a business meeting on the Sabbath, but as I think you will soon see, our town faces an extraordinary situation. Extraordinary. And I mean that sincerely. The board feels it must air the circumstances immediately in fairness to all."

Strider went on talking for a moment about the town ordinances that authorized special open meetings, and the retention of paid employees. Half-listening, Bradley scanned the crowd, seeing the familiar faces. Many eyes covertly watched him with curiosity, uncertainty. He was aware of these, but he was looking for Harding and Windle. Finally he picked them out in a row near the back. He breathed shallowly and returned his attention to Strider.

"—so that we believe this extraordinary meeting had to be called at once, under these provisions," Strider said. He put down the gavel and picked up a sheet of handwritten paper.

"Now. Let me review some facts and the situation now facing this board and this town.

"A few days ago, as I guess all of you know, there were disturbances in our town. Later, it developed that a large sum of money had been taken from a safe at the H. R. Yeager savings and loan company. To this board's knowledge, there was no sign of breaking into the safe. Only two keys existed to the safe. One was in the possession of one John McCollum, a codirector of the farmers' co-operative, and the other was in the possession of one Phil Schmitz, the other codirector.

"After the money was found missing, part of the same money was found in the same McCollum's house or shed, and another part was found at the Schmitz property. This money was brought back to the savings and loan by the town marshal, Mr. Jim Bradley, here present, and deposited in a regular account on behalf of the co-op.

"Mr. Bradley did not file charges against McCollum or Schmitz, known to be friends of his. However, yesterday, he did arrest Mr. Yeager, and is at this time still holding same Yeager in the city jail without filing of a formal charge."

A murmur went through the room, Strider reached for the gavel, and the murmur died.

"Last night," Strider went on, "the board tried to get from the town marshal, in a private meeting, the facts behind the case and the reasons for his actions. The marshal will speak for himself, but the board had the impression that the marshal did not intend to co-operate in any way with our attempt to determine why a prominent citizen was being held captive without charges. Or why the marshal's friends have not been questioned closer when there is evidence against them. Or exactly what is going on that allowed this entire mess to get started in the first place."

Thomas S. Simmons leaned forward. "We asked Jim all these things. He refused to answer. I wanted to make that clear."

Strider nodded. "We want to have the answers. The people

of this town have a right to know. After our session in private last night we voted unanimously—this board—to hold this public hearing. Even a law enforcement officer has to be held accountable to the public and the officials who pay his salary.

"What we intend to do here and now is get to the bottom of this."

Someone in a front row asked, "Are you fellows out to fire Jim Bradley?"

"Not unless we're forced to extreme measures," Simmons replied.

A rumble swept the room and the gavel was pounded. Quiet resumed.

Strider said, "We will proceed to question the marshal in open session." He turned toward Bradley.

Tight with anticipation, Bradley got to his feet. "We have two elected county officials in the room. I'd like to have them here in the front of the room. There are empty chairs along here for them."

"There's nothing better," Strider said, "in the board's view than to have our county attorney and Sheriff Harding take full part in this open-disclosure proceeding." He craned his neck. "Mr. Windle? Mr. Harding? Will you come to the front of the room?"

Amid new buzzes of conversation, the tall sheriff and youthful county attorney came to the front and went, stony-faced, to chairs along the wall flanking Bradley's. Harding leaned over and said something to Jean Reff. She nodded, deathly pale.

Strider used the gavel again. "Now, Jim. The town board directs you to report on the status of your investigation and events leading up to, and following, the arrest of H. R. Yeager."

Bradley took a deep breath. "Before I do that, Mr. Strider, I think I ought to make an announcement of my own. Several, in fact. You've said this fact-finding meeting has certain purposes. I want to announce what I have in mind."

The board members looked puzzled, but all Strider could do was nod.

"One," Bradley said. "Before noon today, if this hearing is over by then, I'll file charges of embezzlement and fraud against Yeager. I've already talked about this with the county attorney. Two. A murder charge will be filed against another individual in the death of a man who worked for Sam Kane, a man known as Paul Lars. Three. I intend to seek a petition asking for a county grand jury investigation into this whole matter, and I have evidence to present against other individuals when the grand jury is convened."

Over the buzz of voices he added, "Since the town board chose to have this public hearing, I intend to make some of that material available here and now."

Strider's face went red, then pale. He glanced at Simmons and Bailey, then around the room. Bradley was watching Simmons closely, and thought he saw a flash of fear in the man's eyes. Bailey appeared mystified.

Strider found his voice. "If you have evidence, we want to hear it."

"On Tuesday night," Bradley began, "there was an apparent attempt to break into Tuck's store here in town. While I was investigating that, there was a mysterious disturbance—shooting—near the old park. Almost at the same time, an old shed caught fire. People know that.

"While I was going from the park to the fire, cutting across the fields, somebody took some shots at me and pinned me down in one of those old buff wallows out there. The man escaped. I went on to the fire, and later I investigated the embers and found evidence that the fire had been set."

"Set!" Bailey gasped.

"Kerosene-soaked rags," Bradley told him, aware of the silence in the room as men strained for every word.

Strider said, "If this has any connection with the business at hand, I fail to see—"

"Later," Bradley cut in, "Mr. Yeager showed me pry-bar

marks on the window of the side of his building. He couldn't see that anything was missing. Then, though, when Schmitz and McCollum came to get money from their private safe in Yeager's office for the co-operative, it was empty.

"All of this was very confusing. Yeager said there were no other keys to the safe, that McCollum and Schmitz had them both. They swore they hadn't let the keys out of their sight. This made it look like they had to have been involved in taking the co-op's money.

"A couple of other things happened. Paul Lars came into my office. He had been shot, was in bad shape. He started to try to tell me something. He was the one who had done at least some of the things Tuesday night. He didn't get to tell it all. Somebody shot him again from the door of my office and got away. This time he was dead, as you all know."

"If Lars was guilty," Bailey began excitedly, "and there was someone else—"

"A few more things," Bradley broke in again. "When this board met, one of the things it asked for, and got, was a search warrant for my office and house. That sounded logical. By that time the story was circulating that the loot from Yeager's had been found at McCollum's and Schmitz's farms. I had returned it to Yeager's big safe myself—"

"Was that report true?" Simmons asked. "Did you find the money on their properties?"

"Yes."

The room erupted.

Strider hammered the gavel. "We'll have quiet! Quiet!"

"Do you mean," Simmons asked, "that you indeed did find the money hidden on your friends' properties, but instead of arresting *them,* you came to town and arrested Mr. Yeager, an innocent bystander?"

"McCollum took me to the money, the part of it that was hidden in his shed," Bradley said. He had the feeling that rumors and half-truths had given much of this information to most of the people who were again listening intently. "It made no sense for McCollum or Schmitz to steal money, then hide it, then lead me to it."

"They panicked," Strider said, scowling.

"A couple more things," Bradley went on, ignoring him. "Before the board's search started last night, I got to thinking about why a search might be considered necessary . . . or profitable. I decided to check my office ahead of the search."

"Do I hear you saying," Simmons said, "that you set out to hide any bona fide evidence that might be on your premises?"

"In my office safe," Bradley said, "I found a slip of paper that was supposed to be a note implicating me in stealing the money." Over the hum in the room he went on, "The note had been planted there."

"I suppose you have evidence to support that contention?" Strider asked.

"I want to see the note," Simmons said.

"There was only one person who could have planted the note in my safe," Bradley went on. "I can identify when he did it and how he did it. I can also prove that he killed Paul Lars."

"Who is this person?" Bailey asked over the noise, while Simmons and Strider exchanged amazed looks.

It was part of Bradley's plan to save this for a little while, so he ignored the question. "From the start, the problem has been how someone got into that private safe at Yeager's office. He said there was no third key. I sent a wire to the safe company to see if anybody had ordered a duplicate off the serial number lately, but no one had."

"It appears to me," Simmons, who was now rather pale, said, "that your evidence still points to your own friends. This is what the board is intent on finding out, and—"

"There was a third key," Bradley interrupted.

"That's supposition on your part of course," Simmons said.

Bradley had to smile. "No, sir. There was something from that first night that I had forgotten. I saw a certain citizen of this town out behind his business establishment during all the confusion, routinely throwing away trash—or so it appeared."

Simmons's face lost its last color.

"It was an odd thing for him to be doing," Bradley continued, "but it wasn't until last night that I realized what he might really be getting rid of was *a third key* to the safe in Yeager's office."

"This is nonsense," Simmons muttered. "I think this board has been played with and insulted long enough. I move—"

"This is the key," Bradley said, taking the object from his pocket and holding it aloft.

"Do you know that key is actually a key to the small safe?" Strider asked over the hubbub. "If it is, then this board should recess and this matter should be contested in a court of law. Our business is—"

"You called the meeting," Bradley shot back. "You were the one who wanted the citizens of this town to have the facts. Let's *give* them the facts!"

There was a general uproar in the room as men were asking each other questions, talking at the same time. Strider and Simmons appeared to be in a state of near panic. Bailey simply did not understand, and showed it. Bradley picked Sam Kane out of the crowd and saw the slits of his eyes, the sudden realization of how things had begun swiftly to turn for him. Kane signaled a man who evidently worked for him. The man moved through the crowd and bent over Kane's shoulder. Kane whispered urgently.

"We haven't heard a shred of real evidence," Strider said, banging the gavel. "Be quiet in this hearing! We haven't heard anything new, not a scrap of real proof of anything. Now you come in here with this wild story about accomplices who have yet to be named—"

"I'm going to name them right now," Bradley said.

He paused to let the silence sink in. As he did so, he saw movement at the back of the room and spotted John McCollum and some of his friends pressing in along the wall to join the crowd. Bradley was glad McCollum could be here for this.

"Two things have changed in Emerald Canyon this summer," he went on. "The farmers' co-operative, for one. And I was named the new marshal. Both these factors have threatened the balance of power. New economic things have happened. I've been . . . independent.

"This whole business has been an attempt to discredit the co-operative, wreck it, and get rid of me."

"Do you really think," Strider blustered, "you or the co-operative are that important around here? This is crazy talk! Emerald Canyon was here and thriving before both of you, and it will outlive every man in this room! I for one say I've heard enough of this nonsense, this character assassination by innuendo, and I—"

"This key," Bradley broke in, raising his voice, "was thrown into the abandoned water well behind the unit block of Main Street by Tom Simmons." Voices began to rise, but he kept going. "He got it from Yeager, who used it to open the safe and take the co-op's money. I dug the key out of Simmons's well late last night. It has a mark on it showing it was made at Caldwell's lock shop in Springer. We can find out from Caldwell who had it made—it's still bright and new and I think he'll remember.

"Yeager's was never broken into. He used this duplicate key, got the money to another person, and gave the key to Simmons to get rid of. The money was split and hidden on McCollum's and Schmitz's properties. Paul Lars must have done a lot of that, too, or else he wouldn't have been shot.

"The man who shot him was the same man who tried to plant false evidence in my safe." Bradley turned and pointed. "Sam Kane's foreman, Bing."

Kane was on his feet while men all talked at once and Strider sat back as if paralyzed, the gavel forgotten.

"This is an outrage!" Kane yelled.

"Strider denied statements by McCollum and Schmitz that

they visited with him during the night of the commotion," Bradley added, and the voices instantly hushed to hear this, too. "I think a grand jury can find witnesses who saw McCollum and Schmitz at Strider's. Which makes Strider a liar. *Why?*

"There are a lot of whys. Yeager had the key made. Simmons got rid of it. Strider lied about McCollum's and Schmitz's whereabouts. Sam Kane's foreman planted evidence in my office and killed a man who had a part in moving the stolen money. Who else was involved, and why? Why did they plan it the way they did? I think a grand jury can get to the bottom of all of it—and a lot more. I have other evidence I can present. There has been a conspiracy in this town and this canyon for longer than I know about, and the same people have been involved in all of it."

"You'll pay for defaming the character of good citizens!" Kane said, his face flaming red.

Windle, the county attorney, was now on his feet. He was young, and his pallor showed the intensity of the pressure he felt, but his voice didn't falter. "I've heard enough. I intend to convene a grand jury here without delay. In the meantime, Sheriff Harding will assist Marshal Bradley in taking steps as necessary to protect evidence and hold parties to this case in the area where they will be available."

The sound of the room which had been up and down in volume a dozen times now really broke. It became instant chaos. The three members of the town board sat stunned, staring vacantly. Bradley turned to speak to Harding, but Jean Reff was there, moving toward him. She came into his arms.

"My God!" she whispered over the roar. "My God!"

Harding put a hand on Bradley's shoulder. "We'd better get back to your office. Mr. Windle wants to get started on some papers right away. Are you going to arrest some of these people in here?"

As much as he hated to do so, Bradley disengaged himself from Jean. "Simmons. And Strider."

"Sam Kane?"

"The grand jury is going to have to develop that part."

"How about this man Bing?"

"I don't know where he is, but—"

"He's here," Jean Reff said.

"*Where?*"

"I don't know, now. But I saw him near the livery right after Mr. Kane arrived in town."

Bradley and Harding exchanged glances. Bing had to be taken. Any delay might allow his escape.

"I'll go for him," Harding said.

"No," Bradley said. "It's my town. He's mine."

"I've heard about him. I'll come with you."

"Sheriff, you'll have to take these other men over to the jail first. And Jean—go find Freddie. Wake him up. Get him over there. I lost a prisoner right in that jail once. I don't want anything like that to happen again."

Bradley started for the crowd and the door that seemed miles away.

Harding grabbed his arm. "You can wait five minutes to go after Bing. Then I can help."

"We don't have five minutes. He might be on the way out of here right now."

"You don't want to face him alone."

"You're right," Bradley said, tasting copper. "Maybe I'll be lucky and not find him before you can get back to join me."

THIRTEEN

The crowd was spilling out into the street, incongruous in their Sunday best during this time of great excitement. In the thickening daylight heat, Jim Bradley avoided a dozen hands that tried to make him pause for questions as he made his way hurriedly down the steps. Once into the street he could brush through the crowd more easily and he hurried, heading south for Jenkins's Livery.

Because of the crowd around the City Building, this part of the street only a block away was eerily deserted. A coon dog pup, grotesquely fat and friendly, rollicked out from under a porch and tried to play by nipping at his boot-tops. He ignored the pup and lengthened his stride, heading for the livery barn that sat at an odd angle across the corner of the street at the end of the block.

It was possible, he thought, that word had already gotten to Bing. It was like Sam Kane to bring his hired gun to town with him, part of his court. Bing, however, would not be allowed to show himself in the hearing room; he would have stayed at the livery, perhaps dozing, perhaps talking with the old man there or thinking his own strange thoughts.

It had all gone far better than Bradley could have hoped. Everything was still up for grabs, but he knew with the part of his mind concentrating on it that the money mystery was broken for good now, and the grand jury would dig deep. The truth would come.

But there was no time for self-congratulations. He had to find Bing. The gunman was a key to parts of it. He had to be stopped now, and held.

As he hurried nearer, Bradley glanced backward over his shoulder toward the crowd in front of the City Building. He hoped to see Sheriff Harding's figure hurrying to join him. He did not want to face Bing alone. It was the last thing he wanted. But there was no Harding. Bradley couldn't wait.

Fifty yards ahead, a man Bradley recognized from the hearing room darted out of the yawning black front doors of the livery barn. He spied Bradley and scuttered off to one side, rushing to get away. He vanished around the side of the barn.

So Bradley knew where Bing was.

There was no other way to handle it.

He walked directly up to the barn. Reaching the front doors, he swung to the right side, paused, then drew his Colt. Flattened against the weathered planks of the wall, he ducked around the door opening and inside, again instantly flattening himself against the wall.

There was absolutely no response.

It was dark in the barn, although sunlight leaked through chinks in the rafters high above. It smelled sweetly of hay and animals. Some horses stalled nearby moved around nervously, clumping the earth. Bradley realized he was holding his breath, and exhaled carefully, his gun at ready.

The two-tiered barn had mounded hay above. It hung over the edges of the upper level in big tufts. The lower level was a broad area, dirt-floored, rimmed by closed wooden stalls. The light was not quite good enough to make out every detail. Except for the movement of horses and the twittering of some birds in the eaves, the barn seemed utterly silent.

Bradley knew Bing was in here.

He stepped away from the wall. His pores shrank with the primitive instinct against self-destruction, but he willed himself to keep moving. He took three steps along the side of the stall to his right, which contained a heavy roan, and then put out his left hand to touch a rough support beam he intended to step around, moving into the central arena.

"Stop there," a voice said quietly.

And very close.

Bradley obeyed.

There was movement along the row of stalls to the right, and Bing stepped into view from the place he had been crouched. Hatless, he appeared ghastly white in a shaft of stray sunlight. The carbine in his hands was leveled at Bradley's chest, while Bradley's own weapon—less effective even at the range of perhaps twenty feet—was partly down at his side.

"Let go of the gun," Bing said. His voice was totally calm, in control.

Bradley let his revolver drop to the soft earth at his feet.

"Walk over here," Bing ordered.

Bradley moved toward him. As he did so, he saw that the stall where Bing had been hiding had the door open, and a saddle had already been thrown over the black geld inside.

"I'm leaving," Bing said. "You stand right there. That's far enough. Don't move at all."

"They'll just come after you," Bradley said.

"Shut up." With one hand, Bing jerked straps on the saddle. "Harding is on his way down here right now."

"I said shut up!"

Again Bradley obeyed. He was trying to sort out the probabilities. He did not want Harding to walk into the same trap that circumstances had forced him to test. But Harding was not a stupid man. Chances were good that Harding would know how to handle it—if he got here in time. But was there that much time?

Bing was almost finished with the saddle. The horse was restive under the rough treatment. Bing's face glistened with sickly sweat as he worked by feel, never taking his eyes from Bradley. The man from the hearing room had given him just enough warning, Bradley thought, so he might pull it off. It was easy enough to say that the law would pursue. But given even a few minutes' start, Bing had a great advantage. It was a very big country. If he could make it out of the canyon, riding hard every inch of the way, chances of catching him quickly were not at all good.

And Bradley needed him. Parts of the story could only come from him.

"You can move against the stall wall now," Bing said, gesturing with the rifle barrel.

Bradley started to obey.

The sound of hasty footsteps came suddenly just outside the front doors of the barn.

It was incredible, how fast the man was. Bradley simply did not even see the movement. The first thing he really saw was the rifle barrel as it came toward the side of his head, closing with blurred velocity. The metal crashed into his skull just above the left ear and then he saw yellow stars and blackness and a lot of pain and he was on his knees, dazed.

Bing had felled him to have a clear shot at the doorway.

A voice from the doorway cried out, "Bing, for God's *sake!*"

Kane's voice.

Stunned, on hands and knees with blood dripping from his nose, Bradley turned his head just enough to see Kane striding across the open dirt arena.

"He doesn't have a thing on you, Bing! Christ! What have you done!"

"Stay back, Mr. Kane!" Bing said shrilly.

Kane kept coming, totally caught up in his own problems. "Half of what he said about you in there was bluff, Bing. *Bluff!* Let the so-and-so file all the charges he wants! He can't prove a thing!"

"Stop!" Bing said more shrilly, panic touching his voice for the first time.

"Bing, don't be *stupid!* He doesn't have evidence! Don't you see that? Put that rifle away! Let him just *try* to get anything on us! Don't panic and give yourself away, man!"

"It's too late," Bing said. "Stay right there, I said!"

Sam Kane's stolid face set in angry determination. "By

God, you or nobody else is going to panic, ruin everything. You fool! Give me that gun!"

And Kane took another step.

The rifle exploded. Through a gush of black smoke, Kane's face suddenly became etched in consternation and shock. The impact of the bullet striking him somewhere high in the torso hurled him backward, throwing him slightly sideways, too, and then to the dirt.

"Hell!" It was a half-scream, half-sob of utter despair from Bing. But he turned and grabbed the reins of the horse and hauled it out of the stall. He threw his arms over the saddle to leap up.

Somehow, from depths he had not known he possessed, Bradley moved. He lunged forward and up and managed to catch Bing's right foot. Bing was caught off balance and teetered for an instant, then fell back off the horse. He hit heavily against the planks of the stall and the horse panicked, bolting away from him.

Bradley tried to follow up his advantage, but dizziness engulfed him as he tried to leap forward. Bing swung around, clawing for the rifle. Bradley's leap missed and he sprawled beside Kane. Bing was getting to his feet, levering the action of the carbine.

"Hey!" someone shouted.

From the doorway again.

Bradley half-turned. John McCollum was in the doorway, and behind him, a good fifty or sixty yards outside and up the street, Harding was coming at a dead run. Bits of the crowd were coming farther back down the street. And while Bradley saw all *this,* in a strange, dizziness-induced depth of vision that made the spaces between the elements clearer than normal, like pieces on a chessboard, he also saw something else: the way McCollum had yelled, then turned, planted his feet, swung his arm in a *throwing* motion.

And Bradley even saw the object—a rock—in the air.

It hit Bing squarely in the face, staggering him back.

Bradley lurched after him again and got both legs this time. Bing went down more heavily, cursing and fighting back. Something crashed into the side of Bradley's head, but he hung on, thinking of nothing but hanging on, keeping his opponent from having room to work the rifle.

Then he was dimly aware that McCollum had joined in, and maybe somebody else—Harding. It was all very confusing. He got hit again and then there was a thunking noise and Bing stiffened and slid out onto the ground.

Bradley untangled himself and sat up. John McCollum was getting up a few feet away and Harding stood over Bing, just putting his pistol back into leather.

"I *told* you to wait," Harding said softly.

Bradley turned to McCollum. "You throw a mean rock."

"I owed you something," McCollum said with a thin, shaky smile.

"It's paid."

Harding was bent over Kane. "This might not be as bad as it looks. He's alive, anyway. How do we get the doc around here?"

There was no problem. What seemed like half the population boiled into the barn in the next twenty seconds, and the doc was one of them.

FOURTEEN

Then it was Wednesday. Jim Bradley stood on the porch of the City Building with Sheriff Harding. Evening was coming on and it had been another long day. They had started to become real friends in the three days since the town board session and what had happened at the livery barn. They were smoking together, and although the town was still alight with the continuing excitement, people walked around normally, and a horse-drawn hay wagon went by with some youngsters riding in the back the way they always did when their dad came to market.

"It's going to take a long time," Harding mused.

"I didn't know you could empanel a grand jury this fast, though," Bradley said. "Now that they're ready to start hearing evidence in the morning, things will pop."

"No matter what they come up with, it looks like those new elections this fall won't be coming any too soon."

Bradley nodded. "It's the start of a new day in Emerald Canyon."

"You might not prove everything against all of them."

"I know."

"The case against Kane himself is shaky, unless Bing cracks and tells what he knows."

"I know that. And I don't think Bing will crack."

"You don't?"

"He'll go to the gallows with that same sneer on his face."

"Then Kane might get off."

"One of the others could talk."

Harding looked dubious.

"But," Bradley added, "even that wouldn't matter."

"Explain."

"The old combine is broken. Yeager has had it. You were one of the witnesses to what Simmons confessed today. I don't go much for this plea bargaining—"

"Windle got the confession with the offer."

"I know, I know. I was going to say, I don't much go for it, but at least, after his short term, Simmons won't be around these parts anymore. And no matter what happens to Kane, his power is broken. It's a new deal of the deck for everybody. The grand jury will do part of it. I'm betting the elections will do the rest."

Harding chuckled. "Wouldn't like to come to the county seat and be my chief deputy, would you?"

"I guess I'll stay here awhile."

"I was afraid of that."

They smoked in silence for a while.

"Tell me something," Harding said.

"What?"

"Your speech in the hearing. When you tied Kane in, and talked about evidence on Bing. How much of that was a bluff?"

"I knew it was all true."

"But how much did you have evidence for?"

"Damned little," Bradley admitted quietly.

"I thought so."

"It worked."

"I noticed."

From down the street, Jean Reff left the café and started toward the City Building. She was carrying a tray, and of course she looked beautiful.

"Well, it must be past eight o'clock," Harding sighed.

"What do you mean?"

"That woman comes bringing you your supper every night at this time."

"She has a contract with the jail," Bradley said, his face heating.

"You going to marry her?"

"You know a lawman makes a lousy husband."

"Well," Harding said, amused again, "maybe he does and maybe he don't. But I'll tell you one thing. That woman is a awful good looker. Smart, too. And it's a dadblamed shame, the way she waits on you, looks at you with those big eyes, like she was just . . . waiting."

"Waiting?" Bradley echoed.

"For you to pop the question."

"I couldn't do that. It wouldn't be fair!"

"Marry her," Harding said.

Jean approached them. Bradley met her eyes. Behind her smile there was a tremulous longing that not even her accustomed irony could hide anymore.

"I couldn't do that," he repeated huskily. He was suddenly shaky inside, confronted again by the need.

Jean overheard him. "Couldn't do what?" she asked.

Something made it leap out unbidden. "Marry me," he said, and then was astonished.

She did not blink an eye.

"Yes," she said.